All I Need Is You:

A Christmas Love Story

BY: SHANICE B.

TO KEEP UP WITH MY LATEST RELEASES PLEASE SIGN UP TO MY MAILING LIST BELOW…

www.shaniceb.com

BOOKS BY SHANICE B.

LOVE ME IF YOU CAN (1-3)

WHO'S BETWEEN THE SHEETS: MARRIED TO A CHEATER
(1-4)

LOVING MY MR WRONG: A STREET LOVE AFFAIR (1-2)

A LOVE SO DEEP: NOBODY ELSE ABOVE YOU (SPIN-OFF
TO WHO'S BETWEEN THE SHEETS)

STACKING IT DEEP: MARRIED TO MY PAPER
(STANDALONE)

KISS ME WHERE IT HURTS (1-3)

HE LOVES THE SAVAGE IN ME: A TWISTED LOVE AFFAIR
(1-2)

LOVE, I THOUGHT YOU HAD MY BACK (STANDALONE)

MARRIED TO A DEKALB COUNTY BULLY (STANDALONE)

ALL I EVER WANTED WAS YOU: A TWISTED LOVE STORY
(1-2)

FEENIN' FOR THAT DOPE DICK (AN EROTIC SHORT
STORY)

NO ONE HAS TO KNOW: A SECRET WORTH KEEPING

MEET ME IN MY BEDROOM: A COLLECTION OF EROTIC

LOVE STORIES (VOLUME 1&2)

Chapter One

Dec 1st

Karly

I had the picture-perfect life that bitches would kill to have. I was a successful photographer that were paid top dollars to work with the world's highest paid models. I was only twenty-six and I had already made a name for myself.

I didn't just have a career that was thriving, but I also had a relationship that I believed one day was going to end in marriage. Javier was every bitches fantasy. He was tall, slim, dark-skinned, and sexy. Bitches were always throwing themselves at him because not only did he look good, but this nigga was the most top paid DJ in the entertainment industry. Any time you wanted to throw a party, Javier was the one you called.

Javier had this type of charisma about himself. He could sweet-talk any bitch that he wanted and could even coax her panties off her ass if he so desired. His looks, money, and the vibes that surrounded him was what had bitches wanting to be with him, but there was only one bitch who had his heart and that was me.

I smiled as I began to recall the first time that Javier and I first met. Ellie, which was a model that I had worked with in Paris on numerous occasions had invited me to one of her after parties in celebration of her five years of being a model. Javier just happened to be there as the DJ for that night. I can still remember walking into Ellie's mansion and nodding my head to *Travis Scott (Goosebumps).*

I get those goosebumps every time,

yeah,

You come around,

Yeah,

You ease my mind,

You make everything feel fine,

Worry about those condoms, and way to numb,

Yeah,

It's way to drum,

Yeah,

I get those goosebumps every time,

I need the Heimlich,

Throw that to the side,

Yeah.

Our eyes connected and that's when my legs began to move. I walked over to him, gave him a shy smile, and rapped along to the song. When the song came to an end, he stared down at me and quickly licked his lips which made my pussy quiver. He first complimented me on my crème spandex dress and told me how beautiful I was before he asked me my name.

Javier and I talked during the entire party even though the music was blasting from the speakers. When the clock struck three, the party began to clear out, and Javier took that time to start packing up his equipment.

Ellie walked over to where I was standing and embraced me in a brief hug before she whispered in my ear to be careful with Javier because he was a heartbreaker. I brushed off her warning as just another bitch who probably wanted him and wanted to eliminate the competition.

That same night Javier took me home and we ended up fucking. Never have I ever been the type to fuck a nigga that I had just met, but I couldn't resist Javier.

I remember waking up the next morning and rolling over to find the other side of the bed empty. I cursed myself for acting like a damn whore and fucking a nigga that I had just met. In my mind, I knew that giving it up so easy automatically stuck me in the category with all the rest of the thots that he had probably smashed along the way.

I headed downstairs not expecting to find Javier cooking breakfast for me. I had expected to not hear from him ever again.

A year and a half later we were still together and was now known as the most highly paid couple in our social circle. We were making money moves and there was no stopping us from winning.

I had just pulled up at my studio that I used to photo shoot a variety of models and slid out my 2018 candy apple red Audi. I didn't hesitate to zip my jacket up as the November wind slapped me in my face. I hurried to unlock the studio door and rushed inside. I flipped on the lights and turned on the heat as I started to prepare my morning coffee.

I looked up at the clock that was hanging on the wall and was grateful that I still had thirty minutes before Amber arrived. Amber and I had worked together a few times throughout my career. She was soft spoken and easy to work with. The fact that Amber was naturally beautiful with no help from any makeup is how she became famous.

Amber was mocha in complexion, tall, slim, with long black hair that stopped at her ass. She had been featured on the front cover of Vogue magazine as the world sexiest African American model.

Now that she was pregnant with twin girls, Amber had begun to slow down with her workload and was more focused on maintaining a healthy pregnancy. Today was going to be her last photo shoot until she gave birth to her twins.

As the smell of coffee filled the air, I unwrapped a blueberry muffin from off the counter, and started to munch on it as I poured me a fresh cup of coffee. I was halfway done with my muffin when I heard a knock at my door. I sat my cup of coffee down along with my muffin and headed towards the door. I peeped out the peephole to find Amber standing there with her hair blowing in the wind. I stepped back to let her inside.

"Morning Amber, how are you feeling today?"

Amber flashed me a smile before she pulled off her coat and handed it to me.

"I'm feeling okay, just a little tired. This pregnancy is kicking my ass," Amber chuckled as she headed towards the center of the studio.

I hung her coat on my coat rack before I followed her.

"It may be kicking your ass, but you are still looking amazing," I complimented her.

Amber blushed before she ran her fingers through her long dark hair.

"Is there anything that I can get you before we get started?" I asked Amber curiously.

"No, I'm fine, thanks for asking."

I nodded my head at her as I began to get things set up for her photo shoot.

"So, what type of shots are you interested in me taking?" I asked Amber quizzically.

"I'm interested in taking a few nudes. This is my first pregnancy and I want to share it with the world."

"Sounds like a good idea. When you are done undressing let me know."

I headed back into the kitchen and ate the rest of my muffin and took a few sips of my now cold coffee.

"I'm ready to get started," Amber stated a few moments later.

I poured the rest of the cold coffee down the drain before I headed back towards my camera.

Both of Amber's hands covered her perky breasts while her hot pink thong clung to her chocolate skin.

We were only ten shots in when my phone began to vibrate in my pocket. I ignored it and continued to finish the photo shoot. I hated answering my phone when I was with a model, it always fucked up my creativity.

I groaned when my phone started vibrating yet again.

"Amber, can you give me on second," I told her as I pulled out my phone from my black skin-tight jeans.

I didn't recognize the number but decided to pick up anyway. It had to be someone who knew me personally because no one had my personal number.

"Hello," I said into the phone with a little irritation in my voice.

This is the Piedmont Atlanta Hospital, my name is Dr. Holley, I'm trying to get in touch with anyone who is related to Mr. Javier Turner. This number was listed in his phone as his baby sister Karly. I tried calling his wife first, but I couldn't reach her.

"My name is Karly," I spoke softly into the phone.

My heart began to race and my brain began to run a mile a minute. Something wasn't right, I could feel it in my soul.

"I was calling to inform you that Javier has been in a car accident."

I didn't even give the woman time to say anything else as my I-Phone dropped from my hand.

Tears fell down my cheeks and for a minute I zoned out.

"Are you okay Karly?" Amber kept asking me.

I was in such shock that I couldn't even answer her.

I stood there in utter disbelief as she began to get redressed. When she was done, she walked over to me to make sure that I was okay.

It didn't take long for the shock to finally wear off.

"It's Javier, he's been in an accident."

Amber gasped.

"I hope he's okay," Amber uttered.

"I hope so too," I mumbled before I grabbed my keys and pushed Amber pregnant ass out the door along with me.

"I'm sorry about your photo shoot, we can reschedule if you want," I tried to reassure Amber.

"Never mind any of that. Focus on Javier. I'm sure I will be satisfied with the ten shots you just took," Amber stated as she parted ways with me.

I hopped in my Audi and pulled out of my driveway. I swerved in and out of traffic as I began to replay the phone conversation in my head.

Why did the hospital call me and tell me that my number was found under his baby sister in his phone and what the hell did Dr. Holley mean when she said she couldn't reach Javier's wife over the phone?

That phone call didn't make any sense, but I wasn't in the mood to try to play Mrs. Detective at that moment. I only had one thing on my mind and that was to make sure Javier was okay.

∞ ∞ ∞

I pulled up at the hospital fifteen minutes later and hopped out my car. I rushed inside the hospital and asked for the room number of Javier Turner. After I was given the information that I needed I quickly ran towards his room. Tears began to fall from my eyes as I gently grabbed the knob of his door.

"Excuse me, only family members are allowed into this room," a doctor told me as she headed in my direction.

"My name is Karly McAdams, I received a call from a Dr. Holley."

The woman stared at me for a moment before offering me her hand to shake.

"My name is Dr. Holley, I was the one who called you."

I shook her hand as I took in her features. She was a dark-skinned older woman with long grey hair that she had pulled back in a ponytail. She was short but slim and looked to be around the age of sixty.

"Is Javier okay?" I asked emotionally.

"Right now, he's in a temporary coma."

I covered my hands over my face in disbelief.

"How long do you think it's going to take for him to wake up?" I asked sadly.

"He may wake up in a few days or even a few weeks. I know this may sound scary, but Javier will wake up, his brain just needs to heal from the fatal car accident."

I nodded my head as I wiped the tears from my eyes.

I assure you, Javier is in good hands. He has around the clock doctors and nurses checking on him every hour. Now, are you ready to see him?"

I didn't trust myself to speak so I only nodded my head.

"His wife just came a few moments ago. Right now, only you and the wife are allowed in his room."

It felt as if I was beginning to lose my mind because there was no way in hell that Dr. Holley had just mentioned that Javier had a wife, yet again. A few seconds later, Dr. Holley opened Javier's door for me, and stepped aside to let me enter.

I first spotted Javier laid up in the bed with a cast on his left leg with a tube stuck down his throat. As the door closed behind me, a female stood up from her chair, and told me her name was Amira and she was Javier's wife.

She was dressed in a pair of dark blue jeans, a grey sweater, with a pair of grey boots that went up her leg. She was medium in height, light-skinned in complexion, with soft brown hair that was cut in a short bob. She wore no makeup only lipstick. She was naturally beautiful, I instantly saw why Javier chose her to be his wife. She was different from the average bitch that most men found attractive. When I looked more closely at her that's when I noticed a baby bump, my heart seemed to fall from out my chest because I knew it had to be Javier's baby she was carrying.

"What is your name and how do you know Javier?" Amira asked me curiously.

"My name is Karly and I'm Javier's girlfriend," I told her boldly.

The woman grabbed her baby bump and squinted her eyes at me before shaking her head.

"You're his girlfriend and I'm the wife of his three children."

I swear I nearly passed out because this wasn't something that I was expecting. This had to be a dream, this couldn't be real.

"Javier never told me," I whispered.

The woman chuckled.

"Yeah, I believe you on that. He will lie to anyone who will believe him. He lies so much that I'm beginning to think that he believes them himself. You don't mean anything to him, trust and believe that. I accept his flaws and all, but I do admit it gets hard for me when he keeps finding women like you to fall in love with him," Amira replied sadly as she stared down at Javier's still body.

A tear fell from my eye.

"Now that you know who Javier really is, what are you going to do about it?" Amira asked assertively.

"Whenever he wakes up, tell him that we are done," I replied.

"Karly, next time when you fall in love, watch who you give your heart to," Amira advised.

I didn't even bother by responding, instead, I got the fuck from out of that room before I did some shit that I would later regret. If I was a bitch who honestly didn't give a fuck, I would have unplugged his machine and waited for his lying ass to die.

As I headed back towards the elevator and stepped inside, a voice in my head told me that no nigga was worth going to prison for. I held my tears and refused to cry at that moment because I didn't want to draw attention to myself. I quietly began to hum as I tried to soothe myself. When the elevator doors opened, I rushed outside towards my car.

After unlocking my car and getting inside, only then did I let the tears fall. I had been played this whole time and didn't even fucking know it. As I wiped the tears from my eyes, I began to put everything together. All the missed holidays that Javier claimed he had to work were all lies to cover up that he had a whole bitch and kids at home. The fact that sometimes I didn't hear from him, only for him to tell me he was having issues with his phone was yet again a lie he told me when he couldn't talk to me because he was busy with his family.

Never did he try to move in with me and I never pressed the issue because I never wanted to appear as if I was rushing things. Javier only would stay with me certain days out of the week and then he would tell me that he had to go on the road to DJ for some other clients. I never questioned any of it because he never gave me reasons to.

I had been so stupid and naïve the entire time that I was with Javier. I sat in my car for nearly thirty minutes and cried my heart out until I was suffering from a migraine. I was just about to crank up my car and leave the hospital when my phone began to blast *Rich The Kid (New Freezer)*.

I grabbed my phone off the passenger seat and noticed that it was my mother calling me. I started to send her to voicemail but changed my mind and decided to answer it. It had been over two weeks since I had last spoken to her.

"Hello," I sniffled into the phone

"Hey, baby. Are you okay?" My mother asked with concern in her voice.

"No mom, I'm not okay," I sobbed into the phone.

"Baby, what's going on? Talk to me."

"All I want to do is get over the hurt that I'm feeling inside."

My mother became silent on the other end. That only meant one thing she was trying to come up with the best advice to give me to make me feel better.

"Karly, I hate the fact that you all the way in Atlanta. You aren't anywhere near me. I wish that I could get in my car and come see you. I don't know what you're going through, but I do want you to know that I'm here for you.

"I know you're here mom and I'm glad you're in my life."

"Don't let anyone steal your shine. You a Queen baby girl."

"Thank you," I cried into the phone.

"Karly, you should pack you a bag and come spend some time with me and your father. Christmas is almost is here and it would be great to see you. Last year, I didn't get to see you for Christmas."

"I know mom, I had to work."

"I understand that, but sweetie you have to make time for your family. Money isn't everything."

I wanted to get away before I lost my mind. Going back home to Minnesota sounded like the right thing to do. All I truly wanted to do was forget Javier and move the fuck on.

"Are you going to come home sweetie?"

"I'm coming to see you and dad, I promise."

"That's good to hear baby. Hurry and book a flight, let me know when your plane will touch down."

"I will make sure to call you as soon as I pay for a ticket," I told my mom before ending the call.

After getting off the phone, I sat in the car for a little while longer before I finally decided it was time to get the hell out of there. As I pulled out of the parking lot, I decided to head to my one-bedroom condo. I knew that going back home to Minnesota was something that I needed to do to get myself back together. Javier had hurt me to my soul. All I was left with was tiny fragments of what used to be my heart.

Chapter Two

Karly

Luck was on my side as I booked my plane ticket for the next flight out to Minnesota. I shot my mother a text message to let her know that I was catching the early morning flight that was due to leave that next following morning. As I packed, I began to cry. My heart was torn up inside. How could I have been with someone for a year and not know that they were married?

I hurried to wipe the tears from my eyes as I began to shove my winter clothes into my suitcase. The tears blurred my vision, but it didn't prevent me from packing. I pulled a good number of bras, panties, and other personal items into my suitcase as well. After the first suitcase was full, I started packing a few of my favorite winter boots into my second suitcase. It took me no more than an hour to pack what I felt I was going to need, whatever I missed I was just going to have to buy when I made it to Minnesota, I told myself.

I rolled both suitcases to the front door of my condo and headed back to my bathroom so I could take me a hot shower. As the water sprayed down on my caramel skin, I closed my eyes and saw nothing but Javier. Him laying up in that hospital bed broke my heart but knowing that he had lied to me really shattered it. As I began to wash my body down with my favorite bar of Dove Soap, I decided to forget Javier. When I fell in love, I fell deeply in love, but once I realized that the other person didn't feel the same or worse betrayed me, then there was no love for that person anymore. I was angry at him and at myself for trusting him with my heart.

He wasn't worth my tears and I wasn't going to spend any more time crying over a nigga who didn't belong to me. I was a bad bitch and I could get any nigga my heart desired.

Javier wasn't the only nigga on this Earth that had a big dick, I told myself as I continued to wash my body clean.

After I had rinsed the last bit of soap from my body, I had finally made up my mind that I was going to suck this heartbreak up and move on with my life like I always did. I was going to take my ass to Minnesota and spend time with my parents. I wasn't going to bring any of my emotional baggage along with me. This Christmas was going to be a wonderful Christmas for me and I wasn't about to let anything destroy my mindset.

After stepping out of the shower, I wrapped my wet body into a big towel and stared at myself in the mirror. I gave my reflection a weak smile as I began to admire my features.

I was about 5'2, slim, with long black hair that stopped pass my shoulders. My eyes were brown hazel in color and I was naturally beautiful.

As I continued to admire myself, I couldn't wrap my mind around why anyone would want to break my heart. Yes, I was pretty, but I also had a wonderful personality to go along with that.

I unwrapped the towel from my body and stepped into my bedroom as I began to dig out some clothes that I could wear to bed. After putting on a plain yellow t-shirt, I slid on me a pair of black thongs, with a pair of black tube socks that stopped at my knee. I slid into my bed and tried to close my eyes hoping that sleep would come. Just when I was almost near sleep that's when my phone began to go off. I slowly groaned in irritation as I grabbed my phone off the nightstand that was near my bed. I sat up in bed when I noticed it was one of the models sending her prayers that she hoped Javier was okay.

Instead of responding to her message, I put my phone back on the nightstand and fell into a deep sleep.

His hands caressed my body and his lips kissed every inch of me. I moaned as he began to flick his tongue over each of my erect nipples. My honey box began to drip as he slid between my thighs.

"Open up for me love," he whispered to me.

I opened myself to him, he slipped his tongue into my treasure box, which blew my mind. He sucked on my clit rather gently as he fingered me. I whimpered and cried out his name as he pleased me with his tongue.

"I'm about to cum," I heard myself cry out.

As my body released the steady rush of my juices, he made sure to lick every drop of my sweet nectar before pulling away from me. He placed featherlight kisses on my stomach just before he stared into my eyes.

"I love you, baby," Javier whispered into my ear.

"If you love me, why did you lie to me, why did you break my heart?" I heard myself cry out to him.

Just when he was about to speak the blasting of my alarm woke me. I had been dreaming and it was time for me to wake the fuck up. I rubbed the sleep from my eyes and noticed it was six in the morning. I had to get myself together, I had a flight to catch, and I wasn't about to miss it because of a dumb ass dream.

I wasted no time getting dressed. I slid on a pair of dark blue jeans, with a pink long sleeve shirt, with a pair of black boots that stopped at my knee. I grabbed my black and pink sweatshirt out my closet and pulled it over my pink long sleeved shirt. I made sure to put a pair of diamond studs in my ears as well as in my nose and put on my silver necklace that my mother had gotten me a few years back with my name engraved on it.

I pulled my hair into a tight ponytail, dabbed some lip palm on my pink lips, and pulled out my phone to take a few selfies.

After I was satisfied with how I looked, I booked me an Uber who could take me to the airport. Twenty minutes later, the Uber was outside my house, he helped me get my luggage in the trunk and we headed off to my destination. We pulled up the airport fifteen minutes later. I paid the driver and rolled my luggage inside the airport.

After going through the security process, I hurried to secure my seat on the plane. I pulled out my phone and finally decided to do what I should have been done when I first found out the truth about Javier.

I have always been a private person, but there were no secrets in the entertainment industry. It was time I let the people that Javier and I associated with know that we were over with. I wanted to be the one to tell the shit first before people started spreading lies on what they thought had happened.

I typed a short post on Facebook letting everyone know that Javier and I were no longer a couple. The post wasn't even on there a minute good before people started commenting on the post talking about how sorry they were and they hoped we worked things out.

I laughed because if they only knew the half of the story, they wouldn't have even posted that shit. How could anyone make things work with a nigga who was already married?

When the flight attendant told us to turn off all cell phones, I quickly put my phone on airplane mode and stuck my earplugs in my ear. I closed my eyes as **Kodak Black (Spaz Out)** blasted in my ear and sleep found me.

Three hours later my plane was touching down in Minnesota. I was finally back to my old roots. As soon as I stepped off the plane, I spotted my mother waving and calling out my name. I ran towards her and she embraced me in a tight hug.

"How was your flight baby?"

"It was fine mom."

"Your father and I are so happy that you came home. How long are you going to stay?"

"I'm going to stay until you and dad kick me out."

My mother laughed as she grabbed one of my bags and rolled it to her all black 2018 Range Rover.

"Don't say things like that because you know we want you back up here with us. I hate you all the way in Georgia by yourself. I know you work and travel a lot, but have you thought about relocating back here. Your father and I, have a nice three-bedroom, two-bathroom house, that just came available."

"Mom..." I cut her off.

"What baby?" she asked me with concern.

"I will think about it, okay," I told her truthfully.

"That's all I ask of you, just at least think about it," my mother said emotionally as we put my suitcase in her trunk.

The entire drive home we talked and laughed with one another, I was grateful that she didn't try to pry into my personal life. I guess she was just happy that I was home and she didn't want to upset me. I looked over at my mother and that's when I noticed she was beginning to age.

Even though she was aging beautifully, it finally dawned on me that my mother was getting older. Her once long black hair was filled with strands of grey hair and her soft caramel complexion was beginning to show signs of small wrinkles. She still had maintained her weight and was still slim like she has always been when I was growing up. Even though, she was close to being fifty-six my mother was healthy and was living her best life. She spent her days helping my father run their realtor company which was named McAdams Realtor Agency. They were a power couple and I wanted something just as similar. I thought I had it with Javier, but I had been wrong about that shit.

Twenty minutes later, we were pulling up at my childhood home. We stepped out and of course, the Minnesota air hit my ass with a vengeance. I shivered as I grabbed my bags out the trunk and made a run for it towards the front door. My father was already there holding the door open for us both to head on inside.

"Baby, I'm so glad you finally have made it back home," my father said as I stepped inside.

"I'm glad to be home finally," I told my father before embracing him in a tight hug.

My father was a big tall man, dark in complexion, with a bald head. I always use to joke him and call him the big giant because even though he was a big man his personality was gentle.

After talking to my mom and dad for a little while I grabbed my two suitcases and headed up the long flight of stairs toward what used to be my room.

As I entered inside my old bedroom I flopped down on the bed as I took in my surroundings. I was home at last.

∞ ∞ ∞

Later that night, a soft knock at my door woke me from a much-needed nap.

"Baby, are you getting hungry? Your father and I are thinking about heading out to the Chinese restaurant up the road. Do you want to come along or do you want us to just bring you some food back?"

I sat up in bed as I rubbed my hands through my hair. There was no point in coming all this way and not spend time with my family. If they wanted to go out, I was going to tag along. We had a lot of catching up to do.

"I'm coming along," I told them as I slid out of bed.

I headed towards the bathroom that was connected to my room and splashed some cool water across my face. I stared at my messy ponytail and quickly began to comb through my tangled hair before I applied some more lip balm to my lips. The harsh cold in Minnesota always required me to constantly apply lip balm all throughout the damn day.

I was just about to put my boots back on when my phone began to blast *Rich The Kid (Small Things).*

My heart began to race and all the hurt began to come rushing back. I already knew who was calling me without even looking at my phone. I looked down at Javier's number and cursed myself for not erasing it out of my phone. Instead of answering his call I sent his ass to voicemail. I wasn't ready yet. I didn't feel strong enough to hear his voice right now. I was relieved that he was well enough to call me, but everything else, I wanted no part of.

I hated him, but I didn't wish death on anyone. I just wanted to forget him. I hurried to slide my boots on, grabbed my big coat, and slid my phone into my pocket.

I headed downstairs and tried to forget about that phone call as I hopped in the car with my parents. We had just pulled up at the Chinese Restaurant down the road from our house when Javier called me yet again. I sent him back to voicemail as I headed inside the restaurant.

You better leave a fucking voicemail, if you want to talk that fucking bad, I muttered to myself as I slid my phone back into my pocket.

After we had been seated by a waitress, I looked over the menu for a quick minute before I was ready to order. The waitress took our drink order and wrote down what we wanted to eat. As we waited on our food, we all made light conversation about my job.

After we had finished talking about my job, that's when the waitress came with our drinks.

"So, are you dating anyone back home in Georgia? Are you still talking to that DJ boy? Shit, I forgot his name," my dad said as he sipped his Pepsi

I took a deep breath as I stared at my mother and father.

"We didn't work out. We were on two different pages," I managed to choke out.

"Aww baby, I know how it is when you meet someone and find out, later on, they ain't for you. But you're so beautiful, smart, and successful, you going to get your prince charming soon," my mother assured me.

I nodded my head as I looked away from her. I wanted to get off this subject now before I started crying. I promised myself that I wouldn't cry and I was going to keep that promise.

"Okay, enough about me. How is McAdams Realtor Agency doing?" I asked them.

My dad started to beam as he began to talk about how much business he had been getting since he had hired a girl named Lindsey who was also a model on the side. I listened as my mother and father brag about her and how well she did her job.

"Well, I'm glad ya'll have a dedicated worker for the realtor company."

"We ain't met anyone like her. I'm honestly thinking about promoting her in January she deserves it," my mother told my father.

The conversation about Lindsey and how much my parents loved her ended abruptly when the waitress came with our food.

I didn't even know how hungry I was until I took one bite from my plate. We all ate in silence and was nearly halfway done eating when my mother spotted someone she knew.

"Lindsey, Carter, is that you..." my mother said to a beautiful woman who was about to walk past our table with her family.

She was very beautiful and by looking at her I knew instantly that my parents weren't lying when they said she was a model. She was soft brown in complexion, tall, very slim just like a model, with pink full lips, and her hair was cut into a short pixie cut. I stared at her for the longest moment because I was fascinated over just how gorgeous she looked. She was dressed in a pair of red jeans, with a black sweater, and a pair of black long boots that stopped at her knee.

"Karly, this is Lindsey, the realtor your father and I was telling you about, her husband Carter, and their daughter Charity."

I smiled over at the beautiful family as my mother tried to get us all acquainted.

"Lindsey meet our daughter Karly. I was just telling her that you also model."

Lindsey blushed before confirming what my mother said was true.

"Karly is a photographer and works with the top highest paid models in the industry. She travels all over the world," my mother bragged.

I listened as my mother continued to talk about my career to Lindsey and her husband Carter. It didn't take long before my mother started up a conversation about us doing a little project together since I was a photographer and Lindsey was a model.

I wasn't going to lie, Lindsey was drop dead gorgeous and I loved taking pictures of beauty. I didn't think twice about digging into my purse and pulling out my business card with my information listed on the front. I pulled out a pen and jotted down my personal cell number on the back of my business card before informing her to call the number on the back of the card if she needed to reach me personally.

Lindsey stared at me as if she was in a daze.

"Thank you. I have always dreamed of working with a well-known photographer," Lindsey muttered towards me.

I smiled.

"I will love to work with you, whenever you are available," Lindsey stated seriously.

"Baby, I believe that is a good idea, working with someone who is experienced will really bring more attention to yourself," Carter told Lindsey with happiness in his voice.

Everyone agreed in union at what Carter had just stated.

"I'm all for working with you as well, just call or text me when you are available. I will be in town the entire month of December."

"I will be contacting you," Lindsey responded with a sparkle in her eye.

"You are so pretty," Charity said directly towards me.

"Thank you, sweetie, your pretty yourself," I replied.

She was all smiles as she looked from her mother to me.

"What are your plans for Christmas?" My mother asked Lindsey and Carter.

"Um, we have no plans. We were just going to stay home and have a small dinner," Carter replied.

"Why don't ya'll come over and eat with us then. We will love to have you," my mother stated happily.

Lindsey looked up at Carter to see if he was interested in the idea. When Carter told her that he didn't see anything wrong with having dinner with her bosses, my mother beamed.

"Well, we don't want to hold you up. We hope you enjoy the rest of your night, my father said to Lindsey and her husband Carter.

Lindsey and Carter waved bye, as one of the waiters showed them to a table that wasn't far from where we were sitting.

As I ate the rest of my food, I began to finally realize that coming to Minnesota haven't been such a bad idea. It was a much-needed trip and the fact that I had met someone who was an actual model really floored me. I never expected that to happen here. Working always took my mind off anything that was stressful. Coming home to meet someone like Lindsey had me ready to grab my camera and take a camera roll of pictures of this new model. Her beauty was overwhelming and continued to penetrate my mind as I finished up the rest of my meal.

Chapter Three

Lindsey

My life was far from being picture-perfect, but I was living a dream that so many women would kill to live. I was twenty-seven years old and was married to the love of my life. I was a realtor that worked for McAdams Realtor Agency that was run by Karl and his wife Stella McAdams. It was based in Saint Paul, Minnesota. I had only been working there for two years and was already the top paid realtor on the roaster. I was the one that everyone wanted to come to when they were looking for property to purchase because I always kept it real with my clients. I always made sure to look out for their best interest while most realtors didn't. Using this technique, I gained myself new clients and brought even more business into McAdams Relator Agency.

Selling property wasn't all that I did for my income though. I also was a model for Victoria Secrets. Even though I wasn't the highest paid model for Victoria Secrets, I was still making a decent amount of money. Selling property was my main job, modeling was my passion.

Growing up, I always dreamed of being a model, but after being constantly turned down from different agencies, and learning that my mother had throat cancer, I knew getting a stable job was very important. I put my dream on hold because I wanted to be able to help my mother with the treatment that she needed from her doctors.

Never did I ever imagine that one day coming out of Starbucks I was going to run into an agent that was looking for African American models for Victoria Secrets lingerie. Everything began to happen so fast that I could barely keep up. The same year that I landed my first contract with Victoria Secrets was the same year that I met Carter and fell in love.

I had been in and out of relationships that just wasn't working for me. I always ended up getting my heart broke in the process. I always told myself that I gave way too much of myself in my relationships. When Carter came into my life, I told myself that I wasn't going to let him in, but I eventually gave in after Carter made it known that he wasn't going anywhere no matter how distant that I was towards him.

Six months into our relationship Carter got down on one knee and asked me to marry him. The feeling that I got that day was a feeling that I had never gotten before in my life.

I wasn't the only successful one in the marriage though. My husband Carter was a full-time Psychology Professor at the University of Northwestern in St. Paul Minnesota. Everyone loved him from the staff to his students that attended his classes. My husband had this carefree energy about himself and knew how to make anyone look at the brighter things in life even if they were down on their luck.

Carter and I didn't have kids of our own, but we were full-time parents to his beautiful ten-year-old daughter. Her name was Charity and she was a sweetheart. Even though I wasn't the birth mother of her, she still called me her mother. I came into Charity's life when she was only five years old. I was the only mother she knew since her own mother gave her to Carter when she was only a year old.

Still to this day Charity's mother didn't want to have anything to do with her. It broke my heart every time I stared into her eyes to know that her own birth mother had abandoned her, but I always made sure to let her know just how much she meant to me every day.

Like I said earlier, I had a wonderful life, but it was far from perfect, but there were women who would kill to have what I had. I was far from dumb, I saw how other women looked at my husband and I saw the hate that they had in their eyes when they looked at me. I understood all too well why they wanted my husband for their own. He was brown in complexion, sexy, tall, and rocked a low cut with his sides faded. He drove a 2018 Silver Chevy Silverado with chrome rims and dark tinted windows.

All these bitches saw was his good looks, the nice truck he drove, and the hefty bank account they believed he owned.

I already knew most of all his female students had a crush on him. There had been a few occasions that he had to get a few females removed from his class due to them being obsessed with him.

I always laughed to myself, because these girls were way too young to realize that my husband was happily married and wasn't about to risk his marriage on a piece of college ass.

My marriage was the least of my worries. I knew that the nigga I was with would never fuck me over and hurt me like so many of the others before him.

∞ ∞ ∞

I had just pulled up at Charity's school to pick her up when my phone began to blast *Nicki Minaj (Good Form).* I already knew it was Carter calling because that was his ringtone.

"Hey baby," I breathed into the phone.

"Hey boo, I'm just calling to make sure you were able to pick up Charity from school."

"Yes, babe. I just pulled up at her school. I'm waiting on her to come out now."

"Thanks, baby. I would have done it, but I'm working a little late today. I got a student who needed to retake a test that they missed."

"It's okay baby. I understand."

"Thanks for everything you do for Charity and me. You know she loves you right."

I couldn't help but smile into the phone.

"Please, stop all the mushy talk, you got me blushing."

Carter chuckled into the phone which made my soul soar.

"It's Friday night, so hurry home. I'm cooking tonight."

"Yes, I love Friday's. I'm so lucky to have married a woman who can cook her ass off."

I couldn't help but laugh into the phone.

"I will see you when you get home. I love you, baby," I spoke softly into the phone.

"I love you more, drive safely, and make sure to text me to let me know ya'll have made it home safely."

"I will," I sang into the phone before ending the call.

A few seconds later I spotted Charity skipping towards the car. As soon as she slid into the back, she kissed me on my cheek

"How was school today sweetie?"

"It was good mom," she said as she clicked her seatbelt in.

As I pulled out of the school driveway, she began to tell me about her day in school. We laughed and talked until we pulled up at the house ten minutes later. As soon as we stepped inside the house, she ran up the stairs to take off her school clothes. When she came back down, I was in the kitchen preparing dinner for that night.

"What are you cooking mom?" Charity asked sweetly.

"I'm cooking spaghetti, garlic bread, and french beans."

"Yum, that's my favorite. When is daddy coming home?"

"He had to work a little late, but he will be here soon, so we can all eat together."

As I cooked, Charity sat at the kitchen table and continued to talk about her teachers, her friends, and even a few girls who didn't like her.

"Baby, you are beautiful, never let anyone tell you that you're not," I told Charity as I stirred the pot of spaghetti.

"I know I'm beautiful mother, you and daddy tell me all the time."

"And I'm going to continue to tell you this because it's the truth."

Charity smiled at me.

"Thank you, mom."

"What are you thanking me for?"

"For just being here, for being my mom."

I stopped stirring the spaghetti, wiped my hands, and looked over at her.

"Honey, you don't have to thank me for that. I enjoy being your mother. Even though I didn't have you myself, I still love you as I did."

Charity wiped a tear from her eye as she embraced me in a tight hug.

"Promise me, that you won't ever leave me," Charity cried to me.

"Sweetie, I'm not going anywhere. What makes you think I will leave you?" I asked her.

Charity pulled away from me before she began to bite down on her lips.

"I'm just afraid you're going to leave me like my real mom did."

My heart felt heavy because I knew exactly what she was talking about. Charity was ten years old and already she was stressing over the fact of being abandoned.

I quickly pulled out a chair and sat in front of her. I placed her hand in my own and stared at her for a few moments as I gathered the words to try to calm her down.

"Even before I married your father, I treated you like you were mine. After I married your father, I became your mother. No, I can never replace your mother, but in my eyes, you're my baby. There is no way I will ever leave you, sweetie. You are a part of me, Charity. It will hurt me to my heart to ever leave you. No matter what happens, I will always be in your life."

"Do you promise?"

"Yes, I promise."

"You way too young to be worried about such things, but I do understand why you feel this way. Put them worries away, because you're stuck with me for the rest of your life," I told her before tickling her until she started to laugh.

A few moments later the door swung open and Carter called out to us both. Charity face beamed as she ran towards the living room to embrace her father in a big hug like she did every day when he came home from work.

Just watching them from the kitchen brought joy to my heart because I didn't have that when I was growing up. I didn't have the luxury to have a father in my life. I was about Charity's age when my father took his own life. He was mentally ill and was battling depression that my mother couldn't help him get past. To this day, it hurt me to my heart that he felt he had nothing to live for. My mother always made sure to tell me every single day how much she loved and cared for me. She took care of me by herself, worked two jobs to keep a roof over my head, and I was forever thankful. When she was diagnosed with lung cancer five years ago, I did whatever I could to help her with her bills and her treatment. I was there for her until she took her very last breath.

After Carter was done hugging and kissing on Charity he headed towards the kitchen where he placed a kiss on my lips before embracing me in a tight hug.

"How was your day baby?" he whispered into my ear.

"It's perfect now since you're here."

He smirked at me before he started placing feather light kisses on my neck.

"Ewwwww, yall kissing," Charity began to sing.

Carter pulled away from me and we all laughed.

"Okay, so dinner is ready. Who ready to eat?"

"Meeeee!" Charity screamed out.

"Go wash up baby," I told her as I cut off the stove.

Charity didn't hesitate to run up the stairs to complete the task of washing her hands.

"So, have you decided when we going to start Christmas shopping this year?" Carter asked as he began to fix Charity a plate.

"No, I haven't, I don't even know what to get her," I whispered.

"Anything you get her she will be happy with," Carter said to me.

"Yeah, you're right," I whispered back to him.

"Do you still want to go over to my bosses house to eat Christmas dinner with them?"

"I believe it will be a good idea. This will really help both of your careers. So, I say why not," Carter said to me before he kissed me on my cheek.

I already knew he was right. When I took my first look at Karly, I knew instantly that she was the one who was going to really get me where I needed to go in my modeling career. Not only did she have the connections, but she was eager to work with me as well. I had been turned down by many and I wasn't about to let this opportunity pass me by.

"I want you to know that I'm behind you every step of the way with your career," my husband assured me.

"Thank you for supporting everything I do."

"What type of husband would I be if I didn't support? Whatever you want to do, I'm behind you one hundred percent."

When Charity came back down everyone's plates were fixed. We all took a seat around the table and dug in.

"This food is so gooooddd," Charity sang out.

"Thanks, baby."

"Daddy, ain't mom the best cook in Minnesota?"

"Yesss, she sure is," Carter said as he stared over at me.

"Well, I'm glad ya'll love my cooking because ya'll stuck with me," I joked.

"When are we going to put up the tree?" Charity asked.

"We can do it tomorrow since everyone will be home," Carter replied.

"Sounds good to me. Carter, you got to go up in the attic and get everything tonight."

"I will, as soon as I get done eating this fantastic food."

After everyone had finished their dinner, I started making water to wash the dishes while Charity cleared the table. As I washed, Charity rinsed the dishes for me, while Carter headed up the attic to get the tree down.

After Charity and I were done with the dishes we headed into the living room to decorate the tree. It took over an hour to get the tree decorated like we wanted it to be, but it was so worth it.

When Charity began to yarn, I knew it was time to get her in bed. I walked her upstairs while Carter headed to our room. I made sure to brush her long brown hair back into a ponytail just before she slid into bed. As I stared down at her I couldn't help but see her father in her. They had the same brown complexion and the same soft brown eyes.

I kissed her gently on the cheek before telling her good night.

As I stepped into our bedroom, the sound of the water running filled my ears. I hurried to remove my clothes and headed towards the bathroom where I stepped into the shower with Carter. He quickly turned around to face me as our lips connected. He gently bit down on my bottom lip as he pushed me up against the shower wall.

"Where Charity?" he asked

"I just put her to bed."

"Good girl," he whispered into my ear before sucking on my left earlobe. I moaned out his name as he caressed my naked body.

Steam filled the shower door as he kissed and licked on each of my nipples. I gasped when he lifted my left leg and slid between my thighs. He pushed my hand up above my head as he slid into my love box. I cried out in pleasure as he filled me up inside.

"Shit, Carter," I moaned out as he began to slide in and out of my love nest.

"Fuck, you feel so damn good," Carter whispered into my ear as I wrapped both of my legs around his waist.

I held on to his shoulders as he took me for a ride of my life. As soon as I was about to cum, I felt as if I was having an out of body experience. My eyes rolled to the back of my head as I gripped him tightly.

"Baby, I'm about to cum!" I shouted out to him.

"Gone and nut on this fat dick," Carter muttered into my ear as he continued to beat my pussy down.

After I had reached my peak, he placed me back on my feet. My legs were weak as hell, but Carter wasn't about to let that stop him from catching his nut. He pushed my face up against the glass door of the shower and entered me from the back.

"Fuck," I cried out as he slid back into me.

He played with my nipples as he slammed into me from the back. I cried out his name multiple of times as I creamed all over his dick.

He gripped my hair and slammed into me for the last time before he spilled his seed inside me.

"Shit," he moaned as he slid out of me a few seconds later.

I turned around to face him and that's when he placed a kiss on my lips.

"I swear you got the tightest pussy I've ever had. Marrying you was a good choice," he joked just before he pulled me towards him.

"So basically, you married me because I had good pussy?" I joked.

"No baby," he laughed.

"Ummhmm," I laughed with him as I pinched him.

"No one is perfect on this Earth, but you're perfect for me. I married you because I wanted to spend the rest of my life with you. I would have been stupid as hell to not have married you."

"Yes, you would have been one dumb motherfucker if you didn't put a ring on this finger. You not ever going to find a bitch like me again."

"You ain't lied on that. Now turn around and let me wash your back."

I did as I was told and closed my eyes as he washed me. After him and I was both clean, we stepped out the shower and wrapped a towel around our wet bodies. We put on our clothes and slid under the covers for that night. He cuddled up next to me and placed kisses on each of my fingers before staring into my eyes.

"I love you Lindsey and I plan on loving you until I have no more breath in my body."

"I love you just as much baby," I told Carter gently as I stared back into his soft brown eyes.

"Let's get some rest because you already know Charity is going to get us up early in the morning," Carter remarked.

I laughed to myself because he wasn't lying. After the lights were out Carter snuggled up under me. It wasn't long before Carter was snoring. I closed my eyes a few moments later and finally drifted off into a deep sleep.

Chapter Four

Carter

Since I had said the words, "I Do" to my beautiful wife Lindsey I found myself fighting temptation on a consistent basis. The fact that I was a professor and my profession was to teach exposed me to a shit load of sexy college females who didn't give a fuck about my marital status. All they wanted was the dick and all I wanted was to stick. Never had I ever cheated on Lindsey because never did I want to hurt her because she didn't deserve any of that shit. She meant so much to me and had been there for me through so much shit that cheating on her or leaving her wasn't in the plans.

My life with my wife was amazing. She was a wonderful mother to my daughter and a dedicated wife who always put her family first. She was perfect in every way, but I still felt as if something was missing in our marriage.

I was happy with my life, but I still found myself yearning to fuck someone else. Every time thoughts like this crossed my mind, I always tried to push them away and think of what all I would lose if I ever was caught. Did I really want to lose my whole family over some pussy? NO, that would have been dumb of me. There were several students who wanted to fuck me, but I always refrained from fucking any of my students because I knew they could end me if they ever wanted to.

I had just pulled into my parking spot at the college when Renee, the Chemistry professor slid out of her black Honda Accord and walked over to my car. She lightly tapped on my window to get my full attention. I stepped out my car and hurried to zip my jacket up because it was freezing outside.

"Good Morning Carter. How are you doing?"

I didn't even bother by responding, instead, I couldn't help but laugh at her ass. I knew this bitch didn't come over just to ask me how I was doing. The only thing she wanted to know was if I was interested in getting to know her on a personal level. The fact that she had slept with over half of the staff really put a damper on her ever getting my dick.

I loved me a fine ass bitch, but I wasn't into females who was thotish in any way. That was a complete turn off for me. The fact she had slept with half the staff only meant one thing, this bitch was for everybody and that wasn't something I would want to risk my marriage over.

Renee was thick in all the right places, chocolate in complexion, and resembled Blac Chyna. I could understand why so many niggas had fallen between her thighs.

After locking my car door, she followed me into the building, and tried making light conversation with me, but I wasn't giving her what she was looking for. Finally, after ignoring her ass, she caught the hint and left me alone. I headed towards my classroom and hurried inside so I could get prepared for my daily lecture. After I had gotten things situated for that day that's when my door opened, and my morning class headed in and took their normal seats. I waited for everyone to get settled before I started class.

An hour later after my lecture was over, I hurried to pass out the tests that they had recently took a few days prior. After the last test had been passed out, I began to talk to them about their grade because honestly, I was greatly disappointed that only a handful had really passed.

I cleared my throat just before I started to speak on the tests.

"I'm greatly disappointed that there was only a handful of you who passed this test. All of you are very smart students so I know that the partying and drink must have been the issue of why these scores were so low."

I was just about to say more but the bell rung, and the class was technically over.

"Okay, maybe next time we will have more A's!" I yelled out as everyone handed me their test papers and hurried out of the classroom. I was just about to get ready for my second class when I noticed one of my students were still sitting in her chair as if she were in a daze. Tears fell from her eyes and I knew something was wrong.

"Tia, is everything okay?" I asked as I walked over to her.

Tia didn't respond.

I didn't want to press her, so I waited for her to give me some type of answer.

"Have you ever been in love, Mr. Mitchell?" Tia asked weakly.

I froze.

"Why do you ask? What's bothering you?" I asked her gently.

"I'm just curious. Have you ever been in love?" she asked again

"Yes, I'm deeply in love with my wife," I admitted.

She nodded her head at my statement as she lowered her head and cried softly into her hands.

"Just imagine the hurt and the pain you would feel if she ever betrayed you," Tia whimpered.

I stood there because I was trying to figure out what Tia was talking about because she was talking in riddles.

After a few more moments of crying Tia finally wiped her face and bit down on her lower lip.

"I just found out the man who I thought I was going to spend the rest of my life with have gotten another bitch pregnant."

I stood there tight-lipped, not really knowing what to say at first. My heart broke for her because I knew she was torn up inside.

"Tia, I know you're hurting right about now, but things will ease up soon. Telling you not to cry would be wrong of me. Cry long as you need to, but remember you have so much going for yourself, he is the one who fucked up not you."

Tia nodded her head.

"You are the best student in this damn class, very intelligent, and beautiful. You will find someone else who will appreciate you," I promise you that.

"I lost three years that I can't get back. I hate the idea of starting over."

"I understand that, but starting over is sometimes a must. Just take your time and heal your heart. You don't want the next man paying for what he did."

"You're right, thanks for talking to me, Mr. Mitchell."

"You're welcome, Tia. Like I said, things will get better. Don't look at it as a bad thing. At least you didn't marry him."

Tia smiled for the first time and that's when I realized just how pretty she truly was. Tia was thick, medium in height, pecan in complexion, with long black hair that was down her back. Her nails were freshly polished a hot pink and her lips were glossed to perfection. She was dressed in a pair of thick black leggings, tan booties, with a tan sweater that hugged her curves.

I watched her as she headed out my front door. I couldn't help but wonder why a nigga would cheat on her in the first place. I tried to never look at any of my students in a sexual way, but it was always something about Tia that had me wanting to slide between her thighs. I blamed it on the fact that she never seemed to come on to me or even seemed like she wanted to fuck me, plus I loved that fact that she was smart as hell and maintained a 4.0 out of my class. Looking was all I could do, I quickly snapped back into reality when my next class headed inside.

∞ ∞ ∞

Later That Evening

I had just stepped into the house when Charity met me at the door. I played with her for a little while before I headed up the stairs and found Lindsey inside the shower. I pulled off my clothes and stepped into the shower with her. I placed some kisses on her just before she stepped out to let me have the shower to myself. As the water pounded down on my body, I began to stroke my dick in my hand.

I closed my eyes and that's when images of Tia began to resurface from earlier that day.

"Shit," I muttered as I began to imagine myself sliding between Tia's sweet juicy pussy lips.

I squeezed my eyes shut as I continued to stroke my manhood until my seed spilled out. After releasing my nut, I quickly cleaned myself up before stepping out of the shower.

"Baby," Lindsey called out from our bedroom.

"Yeah," I said as I wrapped a towel around my waist and stepped out of the bathroom.

"I just got off the phone with Victoria Secrets they want me to fly to New York to do a photo shoot."

"When you got to fly out?" I asked her quizzically.

"Well, I have to fly out in the next two days. Which will be on a Friday and I will be coming home that Sunday morning."

I rubbed my hands through my low cut and sighed.

"Okay, I got to find me a babysitter to watch Charity because all this week I have to work late we getting things situated for finals next week."

I saw the sparkle in her eyes began to diminish so I quickly grabbed her and kissed her on her cheek.

"Go do the photo shoot. I will figure something out with Charity. I will just get someone I trust to pick her up from school on Friday. I know you been waiting weeks for them to call you for another shoot."

"Yes, I have, but if you don't want me to go…"

"Of course, I do," I told her as I kissed her gently on her lips.

We broke the kiss and the light reappeared in her eyes. I sighed with relief. Never did I ever want Lindsey to feel that I was holding her back on her dreams of being a model. I knew that was her passion, so I tried to support her anytime that I could.

∞ ∞ ∞

The Next Day

As I waited for my class to come in for that morning lecture, I began to ponder on what I was going to do about Charity. Lindsey was always the one who picked Charity up from school when I had to work late. She even took her to school because sometimes I couldn't do that either. These were the times that I wished that I had a mother or father. Charity didn't have grandparents on my side. I didn't even get to know my mother and father. They died in a car crash when I was only a few days old. I was in and out of foster homes throughout my whole life and never bonded with any of them.

My thoughts of my childhood and the situation about Charity were interrupted when my students entered the classroom. Instead, of lecturing and them taking notes I decided to let them watch a movie.

"Okay class, we have been working hard all week long for the finals which will be next Friday. Today, we will be taking a break. It's going to be like a free day for all of you. I got this movie for ya'll to watch instead of listening to me talk all day."

The class began to cheer and chuckled because I knew they were all tired of me talking most part of the class period. I wasted no time by putting on a classic film and sitting back at my desk. Twenty minutes into the movie I heard light snoring coming from some of the students. When my eyes laid on Tia a warm feeling washed over my body and a thought came to my head. Tia was responsible, maybe she could help me out Friday with picking Charity up from her school and keeping her until I got home an hour later.

"Tia, can you come here for a moment?" I asked her.

Tia nodded her head and walked towards my desk.

Her sweet scent filled my nose as she gave me a weak smile. I could tell by how her eyes looked that she stayed up most of the night crying. She wore no makeup and her long hair was pulled up in a bun.

"Tia, I hate to ask you, but I honestly don't have anyone else I can ask," I whispered to her.

"What's wrong?" Mr. Mitchell.

My wife is leaving Friday morning to go on a business trip. I have to work late Friday due to the finals coming up. I need someone who can pick up my daughter Charity from school and sit with her for like an hour until I get home."

Tia stared at me for a quick moment as she thought about what I had just told her.

"I will also pay you as well if you can help me out this one time."

"Sure, I will do it for you. I don't have to work Friday."

"Great let me write down all the information you will need."

After I had given her the address to Charity's school and the name of Charity's teacher, I scribbled down my address.

"Okay, Mr. Mitchell. I won't let you down," Tia assured me.

Chapter 5

Carter

Friday Morning

It was six in the morning when Lindsey's alarm went off. It was time for her to get ready so she wouldn't miss her flight. Just when she was about to slide out of the bed, I pushed her back down.

"Baby, stop playing, I have to get dress. I don't want to be late."

"Shhh, you won't be late," I whispered to her just before I began to suck on her neck.

I pulled her pajama pants down, pushed her legs open, and started sucking on her clit. She whimpered as I pleased her with my tongue.

There was no way I was about to send my wife off for two days without dicking her down. I slid a finger into her honey pot as I made love to her clit. Her moans and cries were music to ears because I knew I was hitting her spot.

When she started begging for the dick, I pulled away from her, and yanked out my manhood. She licked her lips as she slid my dick into her hungry mouth. She sucked on my long pole and caressed my balls until I was about to cum.

"Fuck," I groaned.

I pulled my dick out her mouth and slid between her thighs before sliding into her wetness. I started out fucking her slow, but it didn't take long before the headboard was banging up against the wall. I slammed into her a few times before bending her legs all the way back towards her head and deep stroking her.

"Shit!" she cried out as she creamed all over my dick.

My dick grew harder as I stared into her eyes as I went deeper. I slid out of her a few minutes later and switched our position. I laid back on the bed as she rode me cowgirl style until we both had reached our peak. After spilling my seed deep inside of her, I laid there barely able to move. She rolled out of bed a few moments later and headed towards the shower.

Twenty minutes later, I sat up in bed as I watched her get dress. I couldn't help but admire just how sexy she truly was. Her hair was pulled back in a ponytail and her perfume filled my nose as I walked over to her and placed a kiss on the back of her neck.

"Are you and Charity going to be alright while I'm gone?"

"Baby, everything is under control. I have one of my students picking Charity up from school since she doesn't have to work today. She said she is willing to watch her until I get home tonight."

Lindsey stared at me for a moment and I quickly put her mind at ease. I already knew Lindsey wanted to know who I had found to help me in such short notice. It was best to tell her now than have her all in her head the whole time she was away.

"Her name is Tia. She is very responsible and is an A honor roll student. I trust her to do this small thing for me. I'm also paying her for her time."

Lindsey nodded her head at my statement and told me that she was going to be calling to check in as soon as her plane landed. I grabbed her suitcase, carried it to the Lyft she had called, and placed it in the back seat beside her. I waved her off and headed back to bed to at least attempt to get one last hour of sleep before I had to get Charity up for school.

∞ ∞ ∞

After I had dropped Charity off to school, I hurried to my job in hopes of catching Tia so we could talk. Luck was on my side, as soon as I pulled up in my normal parking spot, I spotted Tia walking towards me.

"Good Morning, Mr. Mitchell," Tia smiled at me.

"Good morning, Tia, how are you doing this morning?"

"I'm doing okay," she responded.

I was just about to ask her if she was still going to be able to help me out when she beat me to it.

"Um, I just wanted to make sure nothing has changed," Tia stated to me seriously.

"Nothing has changed. As soon as class ends, I will Cash App you the payment."

"Ok, that's cool," Tia stated.

"I think we need to at least exchange numbers just in case you may run into any trouble."

Tia muttered off her number to me and thanked me before she headed towards the building.

I watched her as her hips and her ass swayed. I shook my head and instantly started to feel guilty that I was even looking at Tia in an inappropriate way. As the wind began to pick up, I hurried into the building so I could get prepared for my first class of the day.

As the students piled into my class, I did a short lecture and also discussed finals that were going to be taking place that next following week. The class jotted down some of the important things that I was discussing and even asked a few questions. The year was coming to an end and everyone was beginning to stress over the finals. I made sure to go over as much material that I thought they needed to know for the finals before my first class was dismissed.

As the class filed out, I spotted Tia one last time. Her scent filled the air as she walked past me like she did every day. I had to urge to reach out and touch her, but I fought it. I had no clue why I found myself attracted to Tia in the first place. Never had I ever wanted to fuck any of my students, but Tia was an exception to the game.

The fact she never threw herself at me and tried to come on to me had to be some of the reason why I wanted her. We as people always wanted things that were off limits and Tia was just that thing that I knew I could never have.

After my class had emptied, I hurried to cash app her fifty dollars before my second class came in.

I don't know how I managed to get through half the day, but I did. When the clock struck three, I knew that Tia was probably headed to pick up Charity for school. I worked my ass off until around five and that's when I wrapped everything up.

A text came in a few moments later from Lindsey letting me know that she had arrived in New York and was safe inside a hotel room. I shot her a quick text back and was just about to close out my messaging app when I noticed I had a few messages from Tia letting me know that Charity was okay, and they had made it home safely.

As I drove home, my phone began to blast Elle Mae. I already knew it was my wife calling me.

"Hey baby, I'm just calling to make sure you and Charity are okay."

"Yes, baby, we good. I'm headed home as we speak."

"How are things going in New York?" I asked her curiously.

"It's going great baby, I'm enjoying myself and I'm meeting so many people that I can network with to get my career to popping."

"I'm happy for you baby, sale yourself. You got the personality and the looks, it won't be hard for you," I told her truthfully.

"Thanks, baby, well kiss Charity for me and tell her I love her."

"I will baby," I replied sweetly into the phone before hanging up.

After disconnecting the call, I pulled up at the house ten minutes later. I parked alongside Tia's all black Kia and hopped out. I was just about to open my front door when it swung open.

"Daddy!" Charity screamed out from the kitchen.

I headed into the house and almost passed out when the aroma of food filled my nose.

The smell of Tacos made my stomach growl. I looked around and was shocked to see that the messy house that I had left earlier that morning had been reverted back into good condition.

I looked over at Tia and couldn't tear my eyes away from hers. It was as if I was in a daze. The daydream that I was having all in my head went to hell and back when I noticed that Tia was grabbing her jacket and was about to go.

"Where are you going?" I asked her in confusion.

Tia looked back at me before she started to explain.

"Thanks for the fifty dollars, Mr. Mitchell. I'm just about to head home. I cooked Taco's for you and Charity and I did a little light cleaning."

"You didn't have to do all of this. Please stay, eat with us," I heard myself say.

Charity ran out of the kitchen and looked at us both.

"Tia, don't leave," Charity begged.

"I have a lot of school work to complete," Tia said to Charity as she continued to stare into my eyes.

"Don't go please, just one more hour," Charity wined.

Tia pulled her eyes away from mine and stared at my daughter before she finally sat down her jacket and followed us into the kitchen. We all fixed us a plate and dug in. Charity talked about her day and Tia interacted with her perfectly.

When the food was done, Tia grabbed the plates and began to set them into the sink. She was just about to wash them when I walked over to her and pulled her away from the sink.

"You have done enough. Thank you so much, for your help today."

"Your welcome."

I could hear the bathwater running in the distance, so I instantly knew Charity was getting ready for her bath like she did every day after she ate dinner.

"Well, I need to be going," Tia choked out.

When she tried to push past me, I stepped in her way. I could tell by how she had looked at me during dinner that she wanted me. Her desire was radiating off her body the entire time that I had been in her presence.

"Mr. Mitchell," Tia muttered.

I hushed her when I placed my finger on her lips.

"Don't say anything. Your body has been saying everything that I need to know."

"Am I that obvious?" she finally asked.

I nodded my head at her.

She smiled at me.

"What are we going to do about this little crush that you have on me?" I asked her.

Tia stared at me in shock before responding.

"There is nothing that you and I can do. You are married and you're my teacher. I have nothing but respect for you. I don't want to cross any boundaries."

My dick was super hard as I stared at her and heard every word that she spoke. She was so beautiful and so fucking smart. The fact that she wasn't trashy was what I was attracted to the most. I couldn't help but stare at her as she broke a lot of shit down to me. Just hearing her viewpoint of what she thought really had me wanting to give her some of the dick. I felt this way because I believed that she wouldn't go behind my back and try to ruin me. She understood my situation and respected the shit.

I pushed her up against the sink and took a whiff of her sweet scent before our lips touched. My soul felt as if it had been lit on fire as our tongues began to dance with one another. As the kiss began to deepen and as I began to caress her small body, she quickly pushed me away from her.

"I can't do this. I'm not ready to do any of this. I just got out of a relationship. I'm nowhere near over him just yet to have sex. Having sex isn't on my list and having sex with you is wrong."

"Tia, we don't have to have sex if you don't want to. I'm sorry if I disrespected you. It's just something about you that drives me wild."

Tia pushed her hair away from her face before looking at me.

"The only reason you desire me is because I'm not like the rest of them other hoes that use to throw themselves at you. I'm lowkey and always will be. I don't want anyone ever finding out about this," Tia muttered before pushing past me.

She had just put her coat on and was about to head out the door when I pulled her towards me.

I pushed my tongue down her throat as I kissed her with so much passion that it took both of our breaths away.

I pulled away from her first and stared down at her beautiful face.

"If you don't want this dick then I won't give it to you, but at least let me give you some head."

Tia didn't stop me as I pushed her down on my living room couch and slid between her legs. I pulled down her beige leggings and her black thong. I licked my lips as I came face to face with her sweet-smelling pussy. I parted her pussy lips with my finger and wasted no time with sucking and licking her clit while I fingered her. Her soft moans filled my ears as I pleased her with my tongue.

"Yes, right there," she whimpered as I continued to lick and suck on her sweetness. Her juices filled my mouth as I picked up my pace with fingering her.

"Fuck, I'm about to cum," Tia cried a few minutes later.

I continued to suck on her small bud until she finally released her sweet nectar into my mouth. As her juices filled my mouth her cries began to finally die down.

I pulled myself away from her, pulled her thong and leggings back over her ass, before standing up. Tia stood up on shaky feet and fell into my arms. We stood there and held each other until both of us caught our breath.

"That was amazing," Tia finally choked out.

"Good, I'm glad you enjoyed."

I kissed her on her lips for the last time before she finally pulled away from me.

Just when she was about to walk out the door, she turned back towards me.

"Please don't…"

But I quickly cut her off because I already knew what she was asking.

"No worries, your secret is safe with me."

Tia nodded her head at me before heading out into the cold winter air.

Chapter 6

Karly

A Few Days Later...

If this nigga thought for one second that we had something to talk about then he was sadly mistaken. Javier was on a mission to get my attention, but I was avoiding his ass like the plague. Voicemail after voicemail begging me to talk to him and every one of them went unanswered. This nigga had hurt me, I had no clue why he wouldn't leave me the fuck alone.

I was just about to hop in the shower when my phone began to ring. I groaned when I saw it was his number. I was just about to send his ass to voicemail but decided it was time to finally get some shit off my chest.

"Why the fuck you keep calling my damn phone?" I asked angrily.

"Baby, please, just give me time to explain myself. I tried coming by your place, but you weren't there."

I laughed.

"I'm not home. I'm in Minnesota visiting my parents. I don't know why you pulling up at my house. There is nothing to fucking explain. Nigga you lied to me. The whole fucking time that we were together your ass had a whole bitch and kids at home. Your ass is married, and you didn't even think to tell me this shit. It isn't anything that you and I must talk about. Lose my fucking number because there will never be an us."

"I love you Karly and the only reason I never mentioned my family because I knew you were going to stop fucking with me."

"You are so fucking right. So why even play me like that? Why waste my fucking time lying to me like there could ever be an us? You already belong to someone else!" I yelled into the phone.

"Legally I do, but I've fallen in love with you. I want us to be together."

"I'm good on that. I can't even trust you. I'm a lot of things but I'm not a home wrecker. I don't ever want to be responsible for taking you away from your kids."

"Can you just come back home so we can talk face to face."

"I don't have any intention of ever coming back to Atlanta. Now do me a favor and leave me the fuck alone!" I screamed into the phone before hanging up in his face.

As the hot tears began to pour down my face that's when I heard a soft knock at my door.

"Baby are you okay in there?" my mother asked outside the door.

"I'm okay mom," I muttered.

As the door opened and my mother stepped inside, I took a seat on my bed and stared down at the floor.

"I overheard your conversation."

"Is everything okay?"

"Yes, everything will be okay. I just can't believe I let this nigga waste my time like he did."

My mother took a seat beside me and I laid my head on her shoulder.

"Karly, everything happens for a reason. I'm just glad that you are finally back home."

I nodded my head at her.

"That man didn't deserve your love, you have a wonderful heart, you will soon meet that person who will love you as you should be loved."

"Thanks, mom," I replied sadly.

"Don't cry baby, you too pretty to let him steal your joy. Let's get out and go Christmas shopping. It will take your mind off things."

We both stood up from my bed and embraced each other in a tight hug.

"Get dress and meet me downstairs."

After she had left out my room, I headed towards my closet in search of something warm to wear.

After getting dressed I hopped in the car with my mom.

"Where do you want to go first?" my mother asked as she fluffed her hair in the car mirror.

"I heard Target got a huge sale, so I say let's go there. I want to be able to find you and dad something for Christmas."

"You don't have to buy me and your father anything sweetie. We just glad you here. Go shopping for yourself, buy yourself something nice."

I rolled my eyes as we cruised towards Targets. I didn't care what my mother said I was still going to buy her and dad something.

Target was packed so it took a good ten minutes just to find a damn parking spot. After finally grabbing a parking spot, we hurried inside, and went our separate ways. My mother went towards the women clothing while I headed for the lady shoes.

After finding my mother two pairs of boots, I knew that I was going to have to get me a bucket. I grabbed a bucket nearby and went to work with my Christmas shopping.

I had just found me two pairs of booties and was just about to head over to the men shoes to find my father something when I bumped into a familiar face.

"Hey, Karly, how you doing?" Lindsey asked.

I looked up and came face to face with perfection. Her brown skin seemed to glow and her pink full lips were painted a dark purple. She was dressed in a grey sweater dress with a pair of black thigh boots. I stared at her for a few moments as I took in her gorgeous features before I responded to her question.

"Hey, Lindsey, I'm doing good. Me and my mom just here doing a little Christmas shopping."

Lindsey gave me a wide smile before she agreed that she was doing the same.

"I'm sorry I haven't reached out to you just yet. I just made it back home. I went to New York for a photo shoot for Victoria Secrets."

"That's okay. I know you were probably busy."

"Well, we need to make plans because I will love to work with you."

I smiled at her and nodded my head.

"Do you have plans for this weekend?" I asked her curiously.

"No plans," Lindsey replied.

"Perfect. We should meet up for lunch and we can go from there."

Lindsey beamed.

"That sounds like a plan."

"Enjoy the rest of your shopping and see you this weekend," I told Lindsey before we parted ways.

As I strolled over to the men shoe department, I started to look for something nice for my father. After twenty minutes of looking, I finally found him two pairs of shoes that I knew he would love. After I was done shopping, I headed towards the cashier to be rung out.

After paying for my items, I hurried outside, and put my things in the trunk of my mother's car before heading back inside to find her. I spotted her at the cash register paying for her items, so I waited out front for her to come out.

"Did you get everything you wanted?" my mother asked me.

"Yes, I did, and I saw Lindsey in there as well."

My mother face lit up.

"Did you get a chance to speak to her?"

"Yes, we spoke. We're going for lunch this weekend. She is so beautiful and I'm itching to take a few pictures of her," I admitted to my mother.

"She is a sweetheart. Ya'll will make wonderful friends if you decide to stay."

I nodded my head as I helped my mother place her items in the back seat. There was no way I wanted her items to get mixed in with my own.

After we were done putting her things in the back seat, we hopped into the car, and pulled into traffic.

"I've really enjoyed this," my mother admitted as we pulled up at Ruby Tuesday's.

"Let's eat good and maybe catch a movie later tonight," my mother stated cheerfully.

"That sounds good to me," I told her as we headed inside Ruby Tuesday.

∞ ∞ ∞

The Weekend

I pulled up at Sonny's BBQ and waited until I spotted Lindsey's Grey 2018 Mazda. I waited until she stepped out before I slid out of my car.

"I'm so glad we were able to meet," Lindsey said as she walked over to me.

The strong wind hit across my face and I quickly pulled my black scarf around my throat. We headed inside Sonny's and took a seat by the window and waited for the waitress to come and take our order.

When our orders were taken, and our drinks were set in front of us that's when we finally began to start a conversation.

"While I was in New York for my photo shoot, I overheard a model talking about you."

I stopped sipping on my sweet tea and gave her my full attention.

"What exactly did she say?" I asked.

Lindsey smiled.

"Nothing but amazing things about you. To be honest I'm just shocked that you would even want to work with me. I'm not very well known."

I rolled my eyes.

"You don't have to be very well known to be a great model. You have the beauty for it. Everyone has their time to shine. Not everyone blows up quick, but once they do it's a wrap. You are working under a contract with Victoria Secrets and they have so many models that have blown up and have become millionaires. I'm not going to lie, the ones who bring in the most money they are constantly going to call them in for work. If you aren't being called in on the regular it's only because you're a newbie. Once you get over the threshold of being a newcomer you will be getting calls just as much as the ones who have a big name. I have faith in you."

Lindsey stared at me for the longest moment. I couldn't even look away from her penetrating eyes. It was something about her that made me feel all warm inside. Never have I ever been attracted to a female and I never questioned my sexuality until now.

When the food arrived, we dug in. We laughed and talked about where we wanted to be in the next five years. Halfway through the meal, I was eager to get to know Lindsey on a deeper level.

"So, how long have you been married?" I asked Lindsey curiously.

Lindsey beamed.

"I've been married to Carter for five years. I don't have any kids biologically, but I consider his ten-year-old daughter Charity my own. Her mother gave her up when she was only a baby so I'm the only mother that she has ever known. Most people aren't happily married, but I'm proud to say that Carter and I are a very happy couple. We have a great relationship and I couldn't ask for more," Lindsey stated emotionally.

"Does he support your dream of one day becoming an established model?"

"Yes, he has always pushed me on making all my dreams come true. He is very supportive of what I do."

I watched her closely as I slid the last bite of ribs into my mouth.

"Well, in this industry if you're married it's good to have an understanding husband who will be there for you when you need him emotionally."

Lindsey agreed with me before she cleared her throat and started to ask me personal questions.

She bit down on her bottom lip before she finally asked me if I was married or had a family.

I looked up at her and my heart felt as if it had been ripped out my chest. Just thinking back to the man who had betrayed me really brought tears to my eyes.

I guess Lindsey must have noticed that my whole vibe had changed because she quickly apologized and told me that she didn't mean to pry into my personal life.

Even though a part of me wanted to keep the hurt inside another part of me wanted to tell someone. I wanted to get the bad energy out of my soul, so I could move on with my life.

I ran my fingers through my hair before finally getting the urge to finally give her what she wanted to know.

"I'm not married and never been. How my life is looking and how I'm feeling about men, in general, makes me wonder if I ever want to be married."

"What happened?" Lindsey asked slowly.

I closed my eyes and took a deep breath before letting it out. I opened my eyes and that's when I saw the concern on Lindsey's face.

"The man that I thought I was going to spend the rest of my life with is a DJ named Javier. I met him during a social party of a model that I had previously worked with. I thought I knew him, and I thought we loved each other, but I was naïve about a lot of shit. Turns out he was nothing but a liar. He was married the whole time with kids."

"What the fuck!" Lindsey replied angrily.

"Yep, he was married with kids, but you will never believe how I found out."

"Tell me," Lindsey muttered.

"I was in the middle of a photo shoot when I received a call from the hospital. The doctor told me that he had been in a car accident. I rushed to the hospital and that's when I learn that he was in a coma."

Lindsey shook her head in disbelief.

"My whole life changed when I walked inside his hospital room to find his very pregnant wife with him."

"I'm so sorry you had to go through that."

"Yeah, me too," I replied sadly.

"So, what happened next?"

I chuckled.

"His wife told me that I haven't been the only bitch that he had cheated on her with. She wasn't surprised at all. I was devastated, I got the fuck out of there and booked me a ticket home. I needed to get away from Atlanta."

"Do you plan on going back after the holidays?" Lindsey asked curiously.

"I'm not sure. I travel a lot, so I can basically live anywhere that I want to. Atlanta was my home and it was were Javier lived, but how I'm feeling, I don't even want to step back into that fucking town ever again. I just want to forget him."

Lindsey grabbed me by my hand and stared into my eyes.

"You are very successful, beautiful, and have so much to offer anyone who wants to be committed. Fuck Javier and what he did to you. Don't let one man make you give up on love."

As her hands caressed my own, I felt as if a rush had come over my body. Her warmth and concern for me radiated from her.

"Thank you," I managed to choke out.

"I'm speaking nothing but the truth. You can have anyone that you want. Don't stay heartbroken over a nigga who couldn't give you what you needed. I really hope you think about moving back here though. I'm in need of your guidance and friendship," Lindsey admitted.

I couldn't help but blush at her statement.

"You don't have any family in Atlanta, so you might as well come back. I promise not to bug you if you do." Lindsey reassured me.

I couldn't help but laugh as Lindsey began to pout.

"Will you please stop," I laughed as I pulled out my wallet to leave a tip. Lindsey stood up and smirked at me.

"You're beautiful, you should smile more. If you keep hanging around me, I will keep you smiling," she told me sweetly.

I watched as Lindsey grabbed the check that had been left on our table by the waitress. I smacked her hand away and told her that I was going to pay for the dinner.

"No. I got this," Lindsey said as she headed towards the front of the restaurant to pay for our meal.

Instead of trying to persuade her, I grabbed my purse, and waited for her at the front door. I groaned when I noticed it had started snowing outside.

"This will make the perfect day to take a few pictures, "Lindsey said as we both stepped out the door into the cold air.

"If you down then let me know, I ain't got shit planned for later today," I told her.

"In that case let's get to it," Lindsey retorted.

"Meet me at my parent's house around five. They both will be gone to some Christmas play. I will have the house to myself."

"Okay, cool, I will see you then," Lindsey replied.

As I slid into my car, I headed towards the liquor store to pick me up a bottle of Seagram Gin. After paying for my liquor I pulled my car into traffic and headed home.

Chapter 7

Lindsey

I stepped inside the house and spotted Charity watching T.V in the living room.

"Hey mom," Charity said as I closed the front door behind me.

"Hey, sweetie, where your father at?" I asked her.

"The last time I saw him he was out on the back porch," Charity replied.

I was just about to go find him when Charity called out my name.

"Mom, is everything okay with you and daddy?"

"Of course. What made you think that we aren't okay?"

When I turned around to face her that's when I noticed tears were running down her face.

"Mom, I got something to tell you, but I don't know how you going to take it."

My heart began to race and my throat felt as if it was going to close up. I could tell whatever Charity was about to tell me was something serious.

I walked over to her, took a seat next to her, and held her as she started to cry.

"Mom, I love you," Charity whispered through her tears.

"I love you too baby, now tell me what is bothering you."

Charity pulled away from me and stared at me as if she was having a debate in her head.

"Nothing, I'm fine," Charity finally said as she wiped the tears that had fallen from her eyes.

I was never the type to pressure Charity to talk if she didn't want to. Eventually, I knew she was going to tell me what was bothering her.

"If you ever need to talk then let me know," I told her gently as I stood up and headed out the back door in search of Carter.

I stepped out on our patio and there sat Carter nursing a beer in his hand.

"Hey, baby, um, how you doing? Why are you sitting out here in the cold?"

"I'm just out here trying to get a little fresh air."

I shivered because the wind started to pick up. I could tell by how he was acting that he just wanted to be alone with his thoughts.

"Well, I just wanted to let you know that I'm heading over to Karly's house around five. We will be working on our first photo shoot. It's going to be a test run."

Carter sat down his beer and glared at me.

He gave me a weak smile before walking over to me and placing a kiss on my forehead.

"I love you, baby, enjoy your night out," he whispered into my ear before he took a seat back in his chair and started sipping on his unfinished beer.

As I headed back inside, I couldn't help but get an odd feeling that something just wasn't right. Since I had come back home, Charity and her father were not acting themselves. Instead of harping on them too much I headed into the kitchen so I could start dinner. I wanted dinner to be done before I left to go visit Karly.

∞ ∞ ∞

Later That Evening

I pulled up at Karly's house a little after five and was just about to knock on the front door when it swung up.

"Hey, I'm glad you finally made it," Karly said in a cheerful voice as she stepped aside.

As I headed inside the warm heat hit my face.

"This is such a beautiful house," I told Karly as I pulled off my heavy coat and handed it to her.

"Thank you. I spent my teenage years in this house. It has four bedrooms, three bathrooms, with a patio out back. I'm not going to lie, I loved living here when I was growing up," Karly replied.

The fireplace crackled into the distance as Karly placed my coat on the coat rack and headed towards the kitchen.

"Do you want some hot cocoa or a cup of coffee?" Karly asked.

"I'm fine."

When Karly stepped back into the living room that's when I noticed that Karly was wearing a black see through thin sweater that left nothing to the imagination. I tried not to stare, but I couldn't help but notice that she wasn't wearing a bra.

The fact that Karly was so beautiful was the reason why I felt I couldn't tear my eyes away from her. Her long hair was pulled back from her face and her lips were painted a dark green that matched her dark green leggings. I felt as if I was in a trance but quickly snapped out of it when Karly told me to follow her to her bedroom.

As I followed her up the stairs, I couldn't help but notice that she had a sexy shape. She wasn't too fat and she wasn't super skinny. Even though her booty wasn't very big I knew that she had just the right amount that could be grabbed.

Never had I ever in my life been attracted to another female, so when I couldn't take my eyes away from Karly's ass I knew something was wrong. I wanted to smack myself back into reality, but there wasn't any point in doing that. These were my thoughts, apparently, I wasn't thinking logically to even look at Karly in a sexual way, but it was something that I just couldn't control.

As soon as I stepped inside Karly's bedroom, I knew this was all business and nothing else. As long as Karly didn't find out what I was truly feeling then things wouldn't get out of hand. Shid, I didn't even know what I was feeling because never had I ever had this type of feeling about any bitch.

I looked around her bedroom and noticed she had already gotten her camera set up on the other side of the room next to her bathroom.

"Okay beautiful are you ready?" she asked as she played with the camera.

I smiled at her as I walked over.

"Yes, I'm ready. How do you want me to pose?"

"However, you want to pose, it doesn't matter," Karly assured me.

I stepped in front of the camera and placed my hands over my head as Karly started snapping the camera. Karly took around eight headshots before I stepped out of the camera bright lights and laid in the center of her king-sized bed.

"You're so damn gorgeous," Karly muttered as she snapped a few more pictures of me. Ten minutes later Karly put her camera away and ushered for me to come to view them.

"You are really good."

"Thank you luv, I went to the store earlier and picked up some gin. You want some?" Karly asked before she shut off her camera.

I nodded my head slowly as I stared at her.

"Don't look at me like that, I'm not trying to get you drunk and even if you do, you can sleep it off here if you need to. You really need to relax and have a little fun."

As I followed Karly towards the kitchen, I knew that what she was saying was nothing but the truth. All I did was work all day and come home to my family. Rarely did I ever have time to unwind and just have a good time.

Karly had just grabbed two glasses out of her kitchen counter when my phone began to vibrate in my pocket.

When I noticed that it was Carter I hurried to answer.

"Hey baby, when do you think you going to come home?"

"Um."

I looked over at Karly as she began to mix my drink for me.

"It's going to be, later on, I'm really enjoying myself," I said softly into the phone.

"Alright, I just wanted to check on you that's all."

"I'm fine. I will be home soon."

"Love you," Carter said into the phone.

"I love you too."

Karly passed me my drink and I eagerly sipped it.

"Looks like someone has a curfew," Karly joked.

I rolled my eyes as we headed towards the living room and sat in front of the fire.

"I don't have a curfew, he just isn't used to me being gone this long."

Karly chuckled.

As Karly and I talked she kept filling up my glass. Two hours later I was drunk as hell. I looked over at Karly and noticed that she could handle her liquor so much better than I could.

"Omg, Lindsey, you are so fucked up."

I tried to get up off the floor and almost fell. We both laughed until we cried.

"Shit, I'm wasted as hell," I mumbled.

I looked down at my phone and noticed it was only ten p.m. I groaned because there was no way I was going to be able to drive myself home.

Karly held me up against the wall until I had regained my balance.

"Where's the bathroom?" I asked.

"It's down the hallway on the left."

"Do you need help?"

"No, I can manage."

Karly headed back into the kitchen to pour her another drink while I headed down the hallway to empty my bladder. After I had used the bathroom, I splashed cold water across my face hoping that it would kill some of the high that I was feeling, but I was still high as hell. I was just about to cut off the water and head back to find Karly when the bathroom door slowly opened.

Karly stepped inside and passed me a bottle of water and told me to drink it. I popped the cap and drunk half the bottle before I followed Karly back into the living room. Karly took a seat on her leather sofa and signaled for me to come to sit beside her. I laid my head on her lap and closed my eyes as she played in my hair.

"I'm glad that you decided to come over," Karly said sweetly.

"I'm glad I came as well."

I was just about to say more when Karly's parents stepped into the house.

"Lindsey it's so nice to see you here," Stella said as she embraced me in a hug.

"Karly, are you being a bad influence on Lindsey?" Karl asked.

"Noooo, aren't we allowed to have a few drinks?" Karly laughed.

I groaned as I tried to sit up.

"Honey, Lindsey has had too much to drink apparently," Stella fussed at Karly.

"I'm okay," I choked out

Karly's parents only shook their head at one another before making their

way into their bedrooms.

"Well, ya'll enjoy the rest of the night. We are heading to bed."

"Goodnight, Mr. and Mrs. McAdams!" I yelled out as they closed their

door behind them.

After Karly's parents had left Karly continued to caress her fingers in my

scalp which made me fall into a deep sleep.

As her hands caressed my naked body, I couldn't help but moan her

name.

She placed feather like kisses from my neck all the way to my toes

before she slid her tongue into my mouth. Our tongues danced together

as she began to caress her hand on top of my honey pot.

"I want you so fucking bad," Karly whispered into my ear just before

she pushed my thighs apart and slid a finger into my wetness.

I gasped as she made love to me.

My eyes rolled to the back of my head as she flicked her tongue over

my clit.

"Shit," I heard myself cry out.

As she sucked and licked on my pearl she continued to play in my tunnel of love.

When my legs began to shake and cream began to spill out of my love box, Karly wasted no time licking me clean. After she had cleaned me up, she slid her tongue back into my mouth as I wrapped my legs around her waist.

When the kiss broke Karly pulled away from me and pulled me on top of her. Our legs were placed in a scissor-like position as I began to ride her. She sucked on each of my nipples as I popped my coochie on her ever so slowly. She smacked my ass which brought out the beast in me. I started bouncing and grinding on her as she held on to me. She cried out my name, which only made me continue to throw the pussy on her. I squeezed my eyes shut because I could feel a release coming.

"Fuck!" Karly kept shouting to me as I jumped up and down on her wet pussy.

"I'm about to cum," Karly cried out to me.

I slowed down and started to slowly grind on her as I licked and sucked on her big toe. A few moments later her and I both cried out and reached our climax together.

I groaned when I heard my phone blasting *Rich the Kid (Like This).*

I wasn't going to lie, I was sort of pissed. The dream that I had just awaken from was mind blowing and now the high was gone. I was back in reality, and I hated it. I wanted to remain in that dream and never wake up, but I knew I was being unrealistic.

As I sat up, I noticed that Karly was asleep next to me. I grabbed my phone and picked up.

"Baby, its one in the morning, where in the hell you at?" Carter asked.

I rubbed my head as I cleared my throat.

"I'm still at Karly's. We got to drinking and we both passed out on the couch," I whispered into the phone.

"Since when do you drink to the point of passing out?"

"Carter don't start. I was only having a good time. For the first time in a while, I had a good time tonight. All I do is work and come home every day. I never go out or spend time with a friend. Shit, a bitch doesn't even have friends. I love you and Charity with all my heart, but sometimes I just want to get away."

"I understand all that, but next time you decide to get wasted with your so call friend don't forget to call me to let me know," Carter replied with an attitude.

Just when I was about to smooth things over, he hung up on me. I sat there and stared at my phone in disbelief. I started to call him back, but when Karly asked me if I was okay I quickly placed my phone down on the coffee table and gave her my full attention.

"Yes, I'm fine. It was just Carter he pissed I didn't come home. Never have I ever done this, so he's upset."

Karly shook her head at me before she stared into my eyes.

"As long as you enjoyed yourself you have no right to apologize for being over here and unwinding. There is no way you are going to be my best friend and be all work and no play. How can you ask me to stay and not go back to Atlanta when all you going to do is work and not even have time for us to go out and have a good time?" Karly asked.

As I thought back on her comment, I knew she was only being real with me.

"I meant what I said when I told you that I wanted you to stay. We can have so much fun together and you can help me with my modeling career," I told her honestly.

"Prove it," Karly told me.

I felt as if the room was spinning and I was having a hard time breathing. My hands were beginning to sweat and my pussy was beginning to ache for some relief.

I looked at her for the longest moment. The vibe was intense, and I was clueless on what to do next. As Karly began to caress my cheek, I closed my eyes and whimpered softly.

She was so close to me that I could smell her sweet perfume tickling my nose.

When her lips met mine, I felt as if all the air had left my body.

I was craving her and I wanted more. I opened my mouth to her and welcomed her in. As the kiss deepened something seemed to take over my body. I slid on top of her and began to suck and kiss on her neck like this was something I had done before. She placed her hands underneath my sweater and rubbed her hands across my nipples as we kissed.

Even though I had never been with a woman, I already knew what to do.

Karly was going to be the first girl that I fucked with on that level and I could tell by how she had me feeling there was no stopping us once we went there.

Stella cleared her throat which broke the trance that I found myself in. I quickly jumped off Karly and Stella stared at both of us in disbelief.

"Mom, what are you doing up?" Karly asked.

Stella placed her hands on her hips and told us that she was coming to get her a glass of water.

"The real question is what you and Lindsey doing? I'm just going to pretend that I just didn't see what I just saw. Lindsey, you are happily married and can't possibly be doing something like this and Karly I didn't raise you like this."

Stella sighed and shook her head.

She headed into the kitchen, poured her a glass of water before she headed back into the living room.

"Ya'll both grown so I'm not going to lecture either one of you. If this makes ya'll happy then, by all means, do the shit."

"I'm sorry Mrs. Stella," I replied softly.

I hated that she had walked in and found me almost trying to fuck on her daughter. At the end of the day, she was my fucking boss. What she had just witnessed was something I never wanted anyone to see. I just prayed this didn't affect my job and me working for her.

She must have read my mind because she looked over at me and eased my mind.

"Ya'll secret is safe with me and Lindsey your job is safe, if that's what you worried about," Stella told me before telling us both good night.

After Stella had disappeared, I grabbed my phone off the coffee table and was ready to dip the fuck out.

"Where are you going?" Karly asked in confusion.

"Home, I've done enough."

"No, don't leave. You can stay. It's almost one thirty you don't need to be leaving this late."

I grabbed my jacket out of the closet and was just about to put it on when she snatched it out my hand. She pushed me up against the wall and placed her lips on mine. I tried to push her off me, but we both knew that I really didn't want to go anywhere.

When the kiss broke Karly whispered in my ear, "never have I ever wanted someone as much as I want you."

My heart began to race and I felt as if I was high off some type of drug.

"I feel the same way about you," I heard myself say.

I was only telling the truth, it was time that I was honest with myself. I wanted her and I wanted her to want me too. Now that we were both on the same page what did that leave us at? I asked myself.

Karly pulled me from off the wall and grabbed me by my hand.

"We're not going to fuck tonight. We both been drinking, but once we sober, it will be no stopping us," Karly whispered into my ear.

Even though my pussy was dripping wet with anticipation, I knew that she was right. When we made love, I wanted us both to be sober, I didn't want to be under the influence. I wanted to remember every single thing that happened. As Karly laid back down on the couch, I laid down next to her. She held me in her arms until I fell back into a deep sleep.

Chapter 8

Carter

The more I tried to forget what Tia and I had done, the harder it became. Every time I closed my eyes I couldn't stop thinking about her pretty smelling pussy. I knew fucking with her was wrong on so many levels, but I found myself hoping that we could go farther next time. As I rolled over and stared at Lindsey, guilt started to sink in, but even though I felt guilty for lusting after another bitch, I still loved my wife. I kissed Lindsey gently on her lips and headed straight towards the shower so I could get ready for work that day.

As I showered, I had the urge to masturbate but decided against it. I loved my wife and family. I always said that I would never fuck around with no other bitch other than my wife, but what I was feeling about Tia was something that I was going to have to fight. As the hot water poured down on my sex craved body I began to wonder if Tia was still thinking about me. I had sucked and played in her pussy until she had reached her peak, but I haven't heard not one word from her.

After stepping out the shower, I stared at myself in the mirror and that's when reality finally kicked in. I was becoming the very nigga that I always said that I wouldn't become. The first taste of new pussy was making my mind and body weak. I dried myself and headed into the bedroom to find that Lindsey was finally awake. I kissed her good morning on her lips as my mind began to scheme. I wanted Tia again and the only way I could do that shit was if I distracted Lindsey. Never did I ever want her to find out what I was up to because I knew it would kill her inside.

As I began to dress a plan suddenly popped into my head.

"Baby, you should invite your friend over tonight. It's good that you have an outlet other than me and Charity," I told her.

Lindsey seemed to have been caught off guard. Karly seemed cool enough, but I didn't want any bitch to persuade Lindsey to ever forget about her family and her responsibilities. I didn't like the idea of her hanging around with a female who didn't have any responsibilities and came and went as she pleased. Lindsey staying out late and drinking was something she never did, so already I felt her being friends with Karly was later going to bring complications to our marriage.

Right now, Karly was the distraction that I needed, I only hoped that I wouldn't later regret this shit.

"What do you mean? You put up such a fuss about me staying out Saturday night. I'm shocked you want her to come over."

"Well, baby, I was worried about you. Never have you ever done some shit like that. I'm sorry if I came off as controlling. I think her coming here will be better. I got a shit load of work to do this week. Finals are finally here. So, I want to take the day to really knock a lot of the workout. You know I must have the finals graded and calculated into the system later this week. You know I like to be the first to have the grades finished." I sweet talked her.

"Yes, I understand. Well, I guess I can call her over while you at work." I smiled at her.

"Okay baby, well be good. If I'm not mistaken Charity said she is going to spend the night at her friend's house across the road."

Lindsey nodded her head as she watched me finish getting dress for work.

"After I was dressed, I grabbed my briefcase, kissed her on her forehead and told her I was going to see her later that day."

As I headed out the door, I began to feel free. Everything was going to work out perfectly I told myself as I headed to work.

∞ ∞ ∞

"I wish you all the best on your finals. You have the rest of the class period to finish your test," I told my class.

They all looked at each other before they picked up their pencils and flipped over their test papers.

"Remember, don't cheat because if you do, it will lead you to fail this class."

The class remained quiet and that gave me the notion they were deep in thought. I took a seat at my desk and watched them for a few moments before my eyes landed on Tia. My heart began to race and my dick felt as if it was about to swell. She was dressed in a pair of navy blue jeans, a yellow sweater with a pair of yellow booties.

Her hair was pulled back from her face and her big silver earrings dangled from her ears.

She must have spotted me watching her because she looked up at me and smiled. I watched her as she crossed her legs and I instantly knew she probably still wanted me as much as I wanted her.

An hour later most of the kids had already finished their test and left. No one was left but Tia. I eyed her up because I knew the only reason why she was still here because she wanted to speak with me. Tia was the top one in my class. I already knew without a doubt that her taking this long to take the test was all for show. I walked over to her and placed my hand on her shoulder. She looked up at me with her beautiful eyes and told me she was done with her test.

I grabbed her test from her and headed back to my desk where I took a seat. She grabbed her purse and walked over towards me.

She leaned over my desk and bit down on her lip.

"Can, I help you?" I asked Tia.

She smirked at me before replying.

"Yes, you can eat this pussy like you did Friday."

I couldn't help but smile at her comment.

"You miss me already?" I asked her.

"Of course, I do, but I wasn't going to step to you on no bullshit. You never did call or text so I didn't think you wanted to speak to me anymore," she stated.

I stood up and caressed her on her cheek.

"I haven't stopped thinking about you since that day. You could have texted me, I would have responded to you," I whispered into her ear.

Her breathing started to become heavier and I knew I had that effect on her. Her nipples began to harden against her sweater and that's when I realized that she wasn't even wearing a damn bra.

I couldn't take my eyes from her as I took her all in. If I give you what you want, I want you to do something for me as well.

"What you want me to do?" she asked innocently.

"You will see. Can you meet me after school?"

"I have to work today, but I can always not go."

"Don't go, come be with me today."

"Where are we going to go?"

"We can get a room somewhere, just you and me."

"Send me the address and I will be there," Tia told me seductively before heading out the door.

∞ ∞ ∞

As soon as I had secured a room, I hurried to text Tia the address. Thirty minutes later Tia was knocking on the hotel door. I opened the door and quickly pulled her inside. No words were spoken as we immediately began to undress each other. I pulled off her yellow sweater and came face to face with her beautiful titties. I sucked on each of her erect nipples as she moaned out my name. I picked her up and carried her towards the king-sized bed and laid her on top of the sheets. I stood over her and admired her perfectly shaped body just before I began to finish undressing.

When I was completely naked, I laid down right beside Tia and positioned her where her ass was in my face. I didn't have to tell her shit, she already knew that I wanted my dick sucked just as much as she wanted her pussy licked.

As her pretty lips covered my monster dick, I began to lick on her pussy. As I licked and sucked on her clit, she deep throated my dick like a fucking pro. She was sucking my dick so good that she had my damn toes curling. Just when I was near spilling a load in her mouth, I pulled her off me and slid on top of her. I pushed her legs apart as I eased inside her wetness. Her pussy gripped my dick like a glove as I slowly slid in and out of her sugary walls.

Her moans were soft and her breathing was steady until I started hitting her spot. As she wrapped her legs around my waist, I stroked her deeply. Her cries for me to go deeper didn't go unanswered. As I drilled her pussy, she scratched my back and cried out my name. When I got tired of hitting her kitty kat missionary style, I pulled her legs from around my waist and bent them over her head.

"Shit," she cried as I slid my pipe into her love tunnel.

I worked her coochie for a little while longer and gave her some long deep strokes before I slid out of her and pulled her on top of me.

Some of her hair had slipped from her ponytail and she quickly pushed it out of her face as she positioned herself. I placed my hands on her hips as she threw her pussy on me. Her kitty juices dripped down on my rod as she worked her coochie muscles.

I closed my eyes for a moment as she bounced up and down on the dick. I smacked her ass a few times as she rode me like I was a fucking horse. What really floored me and had me bust my nut was when she did a split on my dick. I shot my load into her without thinking twice about it.

After we were both done, I slid my tongue into her mouth and deeply kissed her. When we broke the kiss a few moments later she grabbed my hand and we headed towards the bathroom where we stepped inside the shower. As the hot water splashed over our bodies, she wasted no time by pushing me up against the shower and stroking my manhood.

When she pulled away from her, I was ready to fuck again. I pushed her fine ass up against the shower wall and told her to arch her back. I slid into her and slow stroked into her tight little love box until she told me to fuck her harder.

When she gave me the go, I swear I tried to tear her ass up. I held her tightly as I slammed into her repeatedly.

"I'm about to cum," she cried out.

I grabbed her by her ponytail and slammed into her a few more times before I reached my peak and spilled my cum inside her sugary walls.

We stood there for a moment as we caught our breath.

"Damn, that shit was good," Tia muttered as she stepped out of the shower.

I stepped out the shower right behind her and watched her as she began to get dressed. I grabbed my clothes off the floor and put them back on.

After we were fully dressed, she walked over to me and placed a kiss on my cheek.

"I need to go."

I gripped her by her arm and grabbed her by the waist.

"Text me when you make it back home."

Tia smiled at me.

As she walked out, I stood there in utter disbelief. Now that I had sampled Tia sweetness, I didn't know how to let her go.

Chapter 9

Lindsey

I poured Karly a glass of wine and took a seat beside her on my couch.

"I'm glad you called me to come over," Karly said as she took the first sip of her drink.

"I'm glad I called you as well, Carter's gone and Charity at a friend house, so I was going to be here all alone," I muttered to her as I stared at her freshly painted lips.

Karly must have spotted me because she chuckled.

"I see you fascinated by my lips."

I cleared my throat as I sat my wine glass down.

"I love your pink lipstick," I complimented her.

"What else do you love?" Karly asked seductively.

I bit down on my bottom lip as I caressed her body with my eyes.

"I love everything about you," I spoke honestly.

"Let's keep shit real between us. Never have I ever been with a female, but I want you," Karly whispered into my ear.

"I want you too," I managed to choke out.

I closed my eyes and whimpered when she began to suck on my earlobe.

Karly pulled away from me and had a devilishly smile on her face before she started to pull my red sweater dress above my stomach. She slid my black thong to the side and didn't hesitate to slide two fingers into my honey box. I closed my eyes and moaned softly as she pleased me. I wanted to stop her because Carter could walk in any time, but there was no way that my body wanted her to stop.

"Fuck," I heard myself cry out as she began to finger me faster. She placed her lips on my neck as I tipped my head back. She sucked and licked on my neck just before she placed her hot mouth over my own. I welcomed her tongue inside, as I popped my pussy on her fingers.

I nearly fainted when she slid her fingers out of my love box and replaced them with her tongue. My body began to tremble when she flicked her eager tongue around my clit.

"Shit," I muttered.

She sucked and licked all inside my honey pot until my body began to drip sweet nectar.

She pulled away from me, I pushed my sweater dress down, and was ready to give her some A1 head. I slid between her thighs and pulled off her grey thick leggings and pulled down her red panties.

I rubbed my fingers against her slit just before I pushed her pussy lips open. I wasted no time with flicking my tongue over her clit just before I began to suck on it ever so gently. Her moans were soft at first until I slid a finger into her love box. I fingered her for a few moments as I kissed and sucked on her clit.

"This feels so good," Karly whimpered.

I pulled my finger out of her wetness and licked her up and down just before I started placing feather light kisses over her body. I slid two fingers into her a few moments later and sucked on each of her nipples.

As I finger fucked her Karly was crying for me to not stop. A few seconds later Karly began to yell that she was about to cum. I continued to aggressively finger her until she squirted all over me. I moved away from her and smiled because never had I ever witnessed any female squirt in real life.

At first, I thought I was going to feel some sort of guilt, but I felt none as I watched Karly pull up her panties and leggings. When I stood up to head into the kitchen, that's when Karly smacked my ass.

"Damn, girl," I cried out.

Karly laughed as she followed me into the kitchen.

When she pushed me up against the fridge and started kissing on my neck that's when I heard Carter trying to open the front door. She kissed me for the last time before she pulled away from me and took a seat in the kitchen chair.

"Hey baby, you home? Karly and I are in the kitchen, we up here talking," I said to Carter as he stepped into the living room.

"Yeah, I'm home boo. Have fun with all that, I'm just going to head upstairs, I need a shower. I'm tired as hell."

I watched as he headed up the stairs and waited until he had closed the door behind himself before I looked over at Karly. She stood up from her chair and told me she was heading home.

"You just going to leave?" I asked her.

I slick had hurt feelings because I thought she was at least going to stay a little longer.

"Your husband here now, I honestly don't want to be around you when he around you," Karly replied truthfully as she headed for the door.

I watched her as she put on her heavy jacket, gloves, and hat before I grabbed her.

"You going to text me, right?" I asked her quizzically.

"Of course, I am," Karly muttered just before she placed a kiss on my lips. I didn't want the kiss to end, but I knew it had too.

"Don't go," I heard myself say.

"Come over tomorrow during your lunch break," Karly whispered to me.

"I will be there," I muttered.

I waited at the front door until Karly had slid into her car and pulled out of my driveway.

∞ ∞ ∞

The Next Morning

I groaned when the alarm clock went off. I wiped the sleep from my eyes as I rolled out of bed. I grabbed my phone off the nightstand and made sure to text Mrs. Hammons to let her know that she didn't have to take Charity to school that I was going to come over and pick her up and take her myself.

After sending the text I rolled out of bed and hurried to take me a shower. When I stepped out of the shower to dry off that's when I noticed that my skin was glowing. My skin hasn't glowed in over a year, so I knew Karly had something to do all of this. Just thinking about her made me smile.

As I began to get dress, that's when Carter finally woke up.

"Morning baby," Carter said to me.

"Good morning sweetie," I replied as I slid my thigh boots on.

"What time are you coming home today?" I asked him as I sprayed on my favorite perfume.

"It's going to be a little late baby, I'm sorry. This week will be the last week."

I nodded my head at his statement as I walked over to him and asked him to zip up my dress in the back.

"What you want me to cook for dinner?"

"You don't have to cook anything, I will just get something on the way home."

I stared at myself in the mirror to make sure I was on point before I grabbed my phone and handbag.

"Well I will see you later on today then," I kissed him on his lips and headed out the door so I could pick Charity up from across the street.

As I slid inside my car, I quickly shot Karly a good morning text. I pulled up across the street blew my horn and waited for Charity to come out. After Charity had slid into the backseat I pulled out into the street and headed towards her school. I asked her about her sleepover, but I got little information from her. I honestly was beginning to feel that something was really bothering her. Never was she ever this quiet, she was a talkative and active child, but the past few days I could barely get a sentence out of her.

"Sweetie is everything okay? You have been quiet lately."

"Mom, I have something to tell you," Charity whispered.

"Okay, what you want to talk about honey?" I asked Charity as I gripped the steering wheel tightly.

Charity grew quiet for the longest moment. We were halfway to her school when she finally spoke.

"Mom, do you remember that day you couldn't pick me up because you had left to go out of town."

"Yes, honey, I remember. He told me that he had one of his students that he trusted pick you up that day."

"I liked her at first until I saw daddy doing the nasty with her."

I pushed on brakes in the middle of the highway. Horns behind me blew, but I didn't give a fuck.

"Bitch, get out the fucking road!!!" one man screamed from his car.

I pulled my car to the side of the road and took my seat belt off. I looked back at Charity and saw that she was crying.

"Baby, can you repeat what you just said," I asked her in a low voice.

"The girl, she came over, she cooked, and she ate with us. After I ate, I went upstairs to take a bath. I was coming downstairs to tell daddy that my tv wasn't working and that's when I saw him between her legs and they were doing the nasty on the couch."

My heart felt as if it had been ripped straight out my chest. I tried to reason with myself, but I knew when I looked into Charity's face that she would never lie or make this shit up.

"Mom, I wanted to tell you, but I just couldn't. I didn't want you to leave me."

"Baby, I told you, I will never leave you no matter what happens."

I wiped Charity eyes and kissed her on the cheek before I noticed the time. I hurried to click myself back into my seatbelt and drove the rest of the way to her school in a daze.

When I pulled up at her school ten minutes later, Charity didn't automatically hop out like she normally did every morning.

"Are you still coming to pick me up after school?"

"Of course, baby, ain't nothing changed, I just need to talk to your father about some things."

Her eyes grew big.

"Don't worry Charity, let me take care of all this."

As Charity grabbed her bag and was about to hop out the back that's when I stopped her.

"Baby, did he see you watching them?"

"No, I ran back to my room and closed my door."

I nodded my head at her and told her to have a good day at school.

I sat there in the school parking lot as I tried to get my emotions in check. I mean I felt like I was going to lose it. I picked up my cell to call him. His phone sent me straight to voicemail. I hit the steering wheel with my hand, just so I could take my frustration out on something.

The fact that I couldn't get in touch with Carter drove me crazy. I called Karly in a panic. She picked up after the first ring.

"Karly," I cried into the phone.

"Lindsey, are you okay?" Karly asked me with concern in her voice.

I wiped the tears from my eyes as I tried to explain what Charity had just told me.

"Carter, he cheated on me."

"What the fuck, are you serious?" Karly asked in disbelief.

"Yes, Charity told me this morning."

Karly became quiet.

"Where are you?" Karly asked me.

"I just dropped Charity off. I got to go to work."

"No, I'm going to call my parents and let them know you can't work today. Bring your ass over here we need to talk about this shit."

"Karly you don't have to do all this."

"I don't want to hear that shit. Wipe your face and bring your ass over here."

"Okay," I whimpered into the phone.

After I ended the call, I wiped the tears and snot from my nose before I drove the five-minute drive to see Karly.

Chapter 10

Karly

Just hearing Lindsey crying over the phone broke my fucking heart. Carter was doing what a typical nigga did when he had a good bitch at home. I wanted Lindsey to be happy, but now I knew that her staying married wasn't going to do anything but break her heart in the long run.

Never had I ever thought that I could love a woman in a sexual or romantic way, but when Lindsey stepped into my life, she completely changed me and my perspective.

I wanted to be with her, but Lindsey had shown no signs that she was thinking of leaving her husband for us to be together. Yes, she had expressed she was willing to stay and not go back to Atlanta after Christmas, but we haven't gotten to the part of us being together.

As I laid in bed I began to wonder if it was the right time to tell Lindsey how I truly felt about her. Since Carter was fucking up on her, I felt that she was going to be forced to leave his ass rather she wanted to or not. We all knew when a nigga cheated the first time it was going to be a repeated offense. He wasn't going to stop and I was going to make sure that she understood that.

I slid myself out of the bed, brushed my teeth, and pulled my long hair into a bun on top of my head. I slid on me a pair of black sweatpants, a grey t-shirt, and headed into the kitchen to put on some hot chocolate for Lindsey.

When I heard the doorbell ring, I hurried to answer it.

Lindsey stood on my doorstep and I stepped aside to let her in. After I had closed the door behind her, I embraced her in a tight hug before I headed towards the kitchen.

Lindsey followed me and took a seat at the kitchen table.

"Karly, I have no idea what to do, I mean shit, I feel like the world has ended."

I closed my eyes and said a silent prayer in my head to give me the strength to be honest and upfront with her. I turned around to face Lindsey a few moments later and went in for the kill.

"Are you sure this is Carter's first-time cheating on you?" I asked her quizzically.

"Yes, this is his first time. I'm still in shock because I thought we were better than that."

I bit down on my bottom lip as I took the water off the kitchen stove and poured it into two cups along with the packet of hot chocolate. As I made our hot drink, I tried to give Lindsey the best advice that I could, but it all came out sounding like I was hating what she had with her husband.

"Lindsey, I understand you love your husband and you want to make things work, but I hope you know if you take him back, he only going to continue to do what he wants to do. You said yourself that this is Carter's first-time cheating on you."

"Yes," Lindsey slowly responded.

"Well sweetie, men are going to be men. If they know they can get away with something they will continue to do the shit. See, this was just a test just to see if he could get away with it. You said your daughter caught them in the act, but you haven't had the time to ask him about this incident. I think you honestly need to think about where this marriage is headed. I just don't want you broken-hearted."

Lindsey wiped her face with her hand as I handed her a mug cup filled with hot chocolate.

"I love him, Karly?"

I shook my head at her comment because just hearing her say some shit like that was fucking with my emotions.

"Do you really love him, Lindsey? I mean you have cheated too. I believe it's time for you to reevaluate yourself and what you really want. Do you even want to be with a man?" I questioned.

Lindsey slammed down her cup and stared at me with anger in her eyes.

"What we did was wrong. Even though it felt right, it wasn't right. I want you Karly, but I need my family. I don't want what we did to fuck up what I have with my husband!" she yelled at me.

When she said that shit, I felt as if I had been punched in the stomach. I took a few steps back because this wasn't what I had expected her to say.

Lindsey must have noticed the reaction because she tried to apologize, but I gave her a fake smile and told her to keep her apology.

"I'm okay Lindsey, you don't have to clarify shit or try to apologize. I see how you feel about me and about us. If you had to choose, I see you will choose his ass over me. I thought that you and I had something, but I guess I was wrong."

"Karly will you please listen to your fucking self. I'm married to Carter. We have a family together. I just can't walk out on my family just because I've met someone else that I'm falling in love with."

I shook my head at her.

"Okay cool. Do what you want Lindsey. This conversation is over with."

I placed my hot chocolate on the counter and walked out of the kitchen. I was just about to head to my room when Lindsey cried out my name.

"Karly, I'm falling in love with you, but I love my family, I can't walk out on them."

I turned around and stared at her.

"You aren't married, you don't have a family or a little kid depending on you. You only have yourself."

"Lindsey you act like you can't be a mother if you leave him. Regardless you will always be Charity's mother rather you with her dad or not. I'm not going to fuss with you or any of that shit. If you don't want to be with me then by all means go and try to work your marriage out with your cheating ass husband."

"Don't do this, don't make me choose."

"It's too late, I made the decision for you."

Chapter 11

Lindsey

Tears rolled down my cheeks as I pulled out of Karly's driveway. This couldn't be happening. This all had to be a terrible dream. I still couldn't wrap my mind around the fact that Karly wanted me to choose either her or my family. I loved my family so fucking much, but as I headed towards Carter's job I began to wonder if he loved me the same way.

Could I really get upset and hysterical when I knew that I had cheated on him with Karly? Was having oral sex the same thing as having physical sex, but as my mind began to think this shit through, I concluded that oral sex was still sex. I had cheated just like he had. There was no denying any of this shit.

I pulled up at Carter's job fifteen minutes later and sat in my car as I tried to calm myself down. I wanted to know the truth. I needed to know the facts. I wanted to get this shit settled today, at this very fucking moment. There was no way I could take my ass home after I had found out what I had this morning about the man whom I loved with all my heart. I tried to push the thoughts of Karly from out my head, but I found it hard to do so. I knew I had broken her heart, by telling her that I couldn't leave my family and pursue what we had, I had straight shattered her inside. I loved Karly I truly did, I just was scared. Never had I ever been with a female and never did I ever think that I would want to romantically be in a relationship with one. But here I was caught between my family and the one girl I would have loved to be with if I could. My feelings were all over the place, and I had no way of knowing what to do about them.

After sitting in the car for nearly thirty minutes only then did I slide out and head into the English department building. As I neared his office my heart began to shake and my legs felt as if they were going to give out. I stopped a foot from my husband's office and tried to calm myself down. After I had given myself a small pep talk only then did I open his door.

I stood there in utter disbelief and I felt as if my whole heart had been snatched out of my chest. I was near tears as I witnessed my husband with my own two eyes between another bitch legs giving her head.

I called out his name and immediately grabbed his attention. He quickly pulled away from the little whore and tried to grab me so I wouldn't leave, but I quickly punched him square in the nose which resulted in him falling on the ground with a nosebleed.

The bitch who had been getting pleased from my husband quickly stared at me with big wide eyes. I knew instantly who she was.

I watched her as she hopped off Carter's desk and pulled down her sweater dress. Her eyes met mine and I quickly told her some real shit.

"I should beat the breaks off your ass, but you're not even worth it. The fact you knew this man was married and you still had the nerve to fuck with him is why I don't have any type of empathy for your ass. If I ever see your ass ever again around my husband, I swear to you I will kill your ass. Try me if you want to bitch. Now get the fuck out my face, you nasty little whore," I hissed at her before she ran out the door.

I looked down and that's when I noticed Carter wailing on the floor in pain. I bent down on his level and told his stupid ass to look at me.

"You had the nerve to cheat on me with that little young ass bitch, you had this bitch to pick up my fucking daughter and have the nerve to fuck this bitch in the same house that I live in with our family."

I laughed evilly.

"Ha, you thought I wasn't going to find out about that little incident. Well, I did find out about it, but I'm not even mad about the shit, because you know what Carter, I got some shit to get off my fucking chest. You ain't the only one who can get some new pussy to fuck on, I found someone else as well."

Carter tried to speak, but I smacked his ass.

"Shut the fuck up and listen to me nigga. I gave you my fucking all and this how are you going to do me? You going to risk losing me for a young ass whore."

I chucked to myself.

"Well, I guess we even now. You have been fucking one of your students and I've been getting my pussy ate by Karly."

I saw the expression on his face, but no words left his mouth. I could tell that he was speechless, and I had caught him off guard.

"Don't look at me like that nigga, you heard me correctly. I've been fucking with Karly and do you know what else? She begged me to leave your sorry ass, but I turned her down because I wanted my family. I didn't want to walk out on Charity or you, but once she told me that I could still be a mother figure to Charity without being with you, I was really beginning to think that maybe just maybe I could pull the shit off."

As he stood up off the floor, he grabbed a few tissues off his desk and tried to clean his bloody nose.

I took a few deep breaths as I tried to calm myself down. After I had gotten myself calm only then did I speak again.

"We both have cheated Carter we both have broken our vows; how do we fix this, where do we go from here?" I asked him emotionally.

He pulled the tissue away from his nose and that's when I saw the pain in his eyes.

"I love you, Lindsey. I don't want to lose you."

"I love you as well, but sometimes love just isn't enough."

"You really going to leave me for another bitch?" he asked me in disbelief and anger.

I covered my face with my hand before he screamed at me.

"Answer me, Lindsey. Are you going to leave me for that bitch?"

"If I could I would. She was right. She told me that you wouldn't stop cheating and look at you. You at work eating her pussy. Why stay in a marriage to a man who will never be faithful to me again. I deserve happiness."

Carter took a deep breath and slammed his hand down on his desk which made me jump.

"Lindsey, it won't ever happen again. I will cut all communication with Tia. I want our family."

I looked at him with watery eyes.

Carter walked over to me and grabbed me by my chin so I could look him in the face.

I pulled away from him and took a deep breath before exhaling the air from my lungs.

"I think I love her Carter," I whispered.

"You may love her, but you can never have her," Carter spat at me before he grabbed his briefcase and headed out of his office.

∞ ∞ ∞

The Next Day

We ate breakfast in silence, no one said not a single word. It was so quiet in our house that you could hear a pen drop.

Charity cleared her throat before she complimented me on the breakfast that I prepared.

"Mom, dad, are ya'll going to get a divorce?"

I almost choked on my food because I wasn't expecting Charity to ask something like that.

"Why you ask that?" Carter asked Charity.

Charity stared at us both.

"Some kids in school said that their parents got a divorce because they didn't love each other anymore."

"Baby, don't worry yourself about anything. Your father and I aren't divorcing."

When Carter grabbed me by my hand and began to caress it Charity dropped the conversation on us divorcing. When breakfast had ended Charity ran to her room and closed the door behind her.

As I began to clean the kitchen Carter grabbed me by my arm and pushed me towards him.

"Please forgive me, Lindsey. Let's just move on and start back over."

I looked up into his eyes and nodded my head in agreement. The only reason why I felt like I had to stay was because of my daughter. I wanted to make my marriage work and try to forget Karly, but that was going to be a process that I was going to have to deal with.

I wanted to forget all the wrong that had been done in our marriage, I wanted to start back over just as much as he did.

As he placed his lips on my own a warm feeling rushed into my body. The feeling of love and commitment engulfed me and that's when I knew that we were on the right path of rebuilding our marriage.

Chapter 12

Karly

A Week Later

My mother and I had just pulled up at Kroger's to get some last-minute

items for our Christmas dinner. We were both walking the aisle in search

of some sage so she could make her famous dressing when I spotted

Lindsey with her family. I started to turn around and go the other way, but

that would have been obvious that I was avoiding her. I stood there and

watched her from a distance while my mom busied herself with finding

her the right seasoning. As I stared over at Lindsey, I could tell by her body language and how she was looking that she wasn't happy. Something was off about her, but I didn't have a clue what it was.

It had been one long week, but I had managed to survive it. Not being able to communicate with Lindsey was the hardest thing that I had ever done, but it was a must. I didn't want to break up a happy home, I didn't want to be that bitch. Instead of pressuring Lindsey to make her see that I was the one for her, I decided to pull all the way back and stop fucking with her.

Her calls and texts went unanswered, I did that for a reason. Why should I communicate with a bitch who had made it obvious that she didn't want to be with me? I already had a nigga that had played me and lied to me, there was no way I was going to accept that type of shit from a bitch.

When my mom told me she had found the seasoning that's when Lindsey looked over at us. I cringed inside because she must have heard my mom's voice.

"Hey Mrs. Stella," Lindsey said.

My mom looked up with a bright smile on her face. I didn't even bother by acknowledging Lindsey. Instead, I turned my whole body around and began to act like I was trying to find something.

"You are just the one I wanted to see. Are you and the family still coming for dinner tomorrow?" my mother asked her.

"Yes, we sure are," Lindsey replied.

"Are we going to have lots of pie?" Charity asked.

My mother chuckled.

"There is going to be all the pie that you can eat."

"Yesss," Charity said happily.

"Thanks for inviting us, Mrs. Stella. What time should we arrive tomorrow?" Carter asked.

"We will be eating around two that afternoon. We are eating early because Karly has an early flight back home the next morning."

I turned around when I heard my mother say my name and that's when Lindsey stared at me.

I saw the hurt in her eyes, but I ignored it.

"Well, in that case, we will make sure we on time," Carter replied before he grabbed Lindsey by the waist and pulled her to him.

"See you tomorrow Mrs. Stella," Lindsey muttered before she walked away with her husband and daughter

My mother turned back to me and shook her head.

"I don't know what you and Lindsey got going on, but I don't want no shit tomorrow for dinner."

"There won't be any of that mom. There is nothing going on with us. We just don't talk anymore," I told her truthfully.

My mother huffed before she grabbed her bucket and headed to the self-checkout line.

"What happened, ya'll were so close at one point?"

"I don't want to talk about it," I muttered.

"Baby, I just want you to know that I love you very much, I don't know what you got going on with your love life, but I'm always going to love you regardless. I just don't want you hurt. That's why I told you to leave these married folks alone, but it's going to be okay sweetie. It isn't the end of the world. If it meant to be it will be. When you love someone, you must set them free, she will soon realize where she wants to be. It already looks like she already having some regrets. Just give it time sweetie.

"Sometimes there just isn't enough time to wait on someone to realize something. I don't have the energy to give any more of myself to anyone. I just want to spend the remainder of this Christmas break with you and dad. I got my life in Atlanta that I left in shambles. I got things that need my attention."

"I understand Karly, I just hope it doesn't be a whole year before I see you again."

I gave her a weak smile.

"No mother, I'm not ever going to stay away from you and dad that long ever again."

∞ ∞ ∞

The Christmas Dinner

As I stared at myself in the mirror, I saw nothing but sadness looking back at me. I couldn't believe that I had come all this way only to be heartbroken again. I sighed, as I rubbed the last bit of purple lipstick over my lips. I pulled my long hair into a ponytail as I slid into my purple sweater dress. Even though I was looking good as hell that didn't stop the pain that I was feeling inside. I was dumb to even think that Lindsey would choose me over her family in the first place. I felt tears start to build up in my eyes, but I quickly wiped them away. There was no way I wanted to spend my Christmas crying.

"Karly, you need to get a grip on your fucking emotions. You have to get through this Christmas dinner. After today you will never have to see her ever again," I told myself.

I took a deep breath, grabbed my phone from off the bed and headed towards the living room. I took a seat beside the Christmas tree and watched as my father placed all the gifts that I had wrapped last night under the tree.

"Karly, you didn't have to get me and your mother all this stuff."

I smiled at him before telling him that I wanted this Christmas to be a Christmas they never forgot.

After he had finished placing their gifts around the tree, he embraced me in a warm hug.

"I love you baby girl."

"I love you too daddy," I whispered into his chest.

"Okay everyone the food is done. I just got off the phone with Lindsey and they are down the road from our house. Let's get the table set and let's get his party started."

I followed my mother into the kitchen and helped her set the table while my dad waited on the front porch for Lindsey and her family to pull up.

I felt as if I was about to die inside when Lindsey and her family stepped into the house five minutes later. I tried to act as normal as I could even though it was killing me inside.

I busied myself helping my mother bring the food out to sit on our cherry wood dining room table as everyone else took a seat. When all the food was brought out only then did I take a seat. I was grateful that I didn't have to sit beside Lindsey, but still hated that I had to sit in front of her.

I wanted to move, but then that was only going to cause tension, so I decided to leave the shit alone. After everyone had piled their food into their plates, my father said a long prayer, and then they all dug in.

As everyone ate their food, I picked over mine. I honestly didn't have an appetite and I didn't want to be there.

I had no desire to chit chat but being quiet at Christmas dinner wasn't going to happen. My mother and my father made sure to interact with me and made sure Lindsey did as well. I forced communication with Lindsey since my mother wanted to know how the photo shoot had gone between us.

When my mother started to pry into Lindsey's modeling business I was forced to say even more.

"I just don't understand how someone with so much talent isn't getting the recognition that they need," my mother expressed to Lindsey.

I cleared my throat and that's when I began to speak.

"The only reason why she isn't getting the recognition that she needs is because she doesn't have the connections that most models have. Most of the models who work with Victoria Secrets have been in the business for a long ass time and have established relationships with the higher-ups."

"Now that's a damn shame," my mother stated as she shook her head.

"When my plane touched back down in Atlanta tomorrow, I will make sure to make a few phone calls. I know the right person to talk to get you where you need to go," I told Lindsey truthfully.

My mother smiled.

"Karly, that would be so nice of you," my mother retorted.

Carter sat down his fork and stared at Lindsey and me for a few moments as if he was trying to see what Lindsey was going to say to me.

"Thank you," Lindsey replied weakly.

"No problem," I responded rather dryly.

I wiped my mouth and pushed my chair back from the table, there was no way in hell that I could take another second of witnessing Lindsey and her husband Carter. The faking was just too much for me to bare.

"Mom, the food was very good, but I need to be packing. I have an early flight in the morning, I have to be at the airport at eight."

"Baby, you barely touched your food," my mother said.

"I will eat something later," I replied before I headed to my bedroom to pack my suitcase.

As soon as I stepped into my room, I closed my door behind me, and that's when I finally was able to let the tears fall from my eyes. I cried until my head started to hurt and my eyes were red. I headed over to my closet, pulled out my suitcase, and began to pack up my clothes, shoes, and personal items, all while I tried to calm myself down.

I was almost done packing when a soft knock came at my door.

"Who is it?" I asked.

"It's Lindsey, can I please come in?"

I wanted to tell her hell to the no, but I just couldn't find it in my heart to be cruel. I hurried to wipe my tears and told her she could come in. The door opened, and she stepped inside. She stood by the door and didn't speak for the longest moment. I guess she was trying to find the right words to say to make things better, but there was nothing she could do to make me feel better about this situation.

"I just wanted to talk to you for a few moments."

"About what?" I asked her.

I just want to say thanks for trying to help with my career.

"Your welcome, you got talent, that's something I can't deny," I muttered.

"If you coming to make sure if I put in a good word, then I am. I wasn't lying."

"I didn't come to talk about my career."

"Then why are you here?" I asked irritably.

"I came to talk about us. Karly, I just want to say that I'm in love with you. It took for you to shut me out to realize the shit. I want to be with you just as much as you want to be with me, but at the same time, I just can't leave my family. I can't leave Charity and I can't leave Carter. We decided working our marriage out is for the best."

"Lindsey, it's cool. Be with your husband, be with your family. I'm not going to stick around to cause any issues with what you trying to do."

As the tears began to fall from Lindsey's eyes, I didn't react instead I looked the other way.

"I don't want to choose, but I have responsibilities. I just wished you could just try to see things my way. Please, I want you to stay here. Don't go back to Atlanta. This past week have been hell on me. If you leave, I feel like I will lose it," Lindsey cried.

I looked at her for a moment and laughed at her.

"You are one selfish bitch, you want me to stay here in this boring ass town, just to be here for you. How can I be your friend Lindsey when we both are in love with each other? We killed our friendship when we started fucking around. Why ask me to do some shit like that? I would have stayed if we were going to take this shit to the next level, but you told me you didn't want to leave your family. I'm not about to put my life on hold while you live yours. I deserve to be happy and I won't be if I stay here."

Lindsey wiped her tears from her eyes and began to back away from me.

"I enjoyed the little time that we spent together," she said emotionally before walking out of my bedroom.

After she had left, I zipped my suitcase, laid across my bed, and cried myself to sleep.

Chapter 13

Lindsey

When we left the Christmas party, it was close to six in the evening and it was pitch dark. As Carter drove home, I felt as if I was in a daze. Carter kept asking if I was okay, I lied and told him that I was. I was far from okay, my heart felt as if it was broken into two pieces. My family had one part of my heart and Karly had the other part. As Carter pulled up at our house, I stepped out of the car to find that Charity was fast asleep in the back seat. I shook her gently to wake her. She slid out of the back seat and followed me into the house and into her room. I slid her into bed and was just about to put some covers over here when she stared up at me.

"Mom, thanks for not leaving me," Charity replied sleepily.

I placed a kiss on her cheek.

"I made a promise to you Charity. I'm always going to be here," I whispered into her ear.

As Charity dozed back off into a deep sleep, I headed into my bathroom so I could take me a hot shower. I removed my clothes and stepped inside the shower a few moments later. As the hot water washed over my body images of Karly began to resurface in my mind. I closed my eyes tightly, but Karly didn't leave my headspace. Now that she was leaving, I was going to lose her forever, did I really want that?

I stood there in the shower and continued to let the hot water beat down my body until it was time to get out. I wrapped my body into a big black towel and wiped the foggy mirror with my hand.

Carter stepped into the bathroom a few moments later and placed a kiss on my cheek.

"Lindsey, get out your head. You are making the decision that any female with a family would make."

"I'm not every female," I muttered to him.

Carter sighed before pulling away from me.

"I don't want to force you to do anything that you don't want to do."

He left out the bathroom and left me with nothing but my own thoughts.

∞ ∞ ∞

The Next Morning

I slid out of bed and was grateful that Carter was still asleep. I hurried to throw on me a pair of black leggings, a baggy green sweater with my black booties. I brushed my short hair and made sure to brush my teeth just before I slid on my big black coat and headed out the door. If I wanted to make it to the airport in time, then I needed to hurry up and get my ass there. Ten minutes later I pulled up at the airport and rushed inside. It was packed as fuck, but it wasn't long before I heard that the next flight for Atlanta was leaving out in the next five minutes. I ran towards the terminal of the Atlanta flight and that's when I spotted Karly sitting down with her luggage. She was on the phone with a cup of coffee in her hand.

"Karly!" I called out.

She looked up at me and I walked over to her.

By the time I reached her, she had already ended her call.

"What are you doing here?" Karly asked for a confused look on her face.

"I came to say goodbye. I never did get the chance to say goodbye last night," I choked out.

Tears fell from my eyes and that's when Karly embraced me in a hug.

"Be safe," I muttered to her.

"I will," she told me gently.

I pulled away from her and that's when our lips locked together. The kiss was deep, and it set my soul on fire. Our tongues danced together for the longest time before the kiss was broken.

"I love you," I cried out to her.

"Sometimes love just isn't enough," Karly whispered.

When it was time for her to board her plane, tears blurred my vision

"I just got off the phone with the CEO of Victoria Secrets. You should be getting a shitload of phone calls from now on. I put in a good word for you."

I stood there dumbfounded as I watched her board her plane. I stayed not able to move until her plane had taken off. I headed back to my car and sat there for over twenty minutes. After, I had finally gotten my emotions in check only then did I head home to my family.

Chapter 14

The Epilogue

(Six Months Later)

I had been in Paris for almost three days working with different models for Victoria Secrets. I had done almost ten photo shoots and was just about to get ready to do my last one. I had just finished my morning cup of coffee when the model that I was going to be working with stepped inside the studio. My heart felt as if it was about to fall out my chest when I spotted Lindsey walking towards me. Both of our eyes connected, and I felt the energy in the room beginning to change.

No one seemed to notice it but me and her. She walked over to me, dressed in a pair of Victoria Secrets lingerie. She kissed me on both of my cheeks and embraced me in a hug.

"I've tried calling you and texting you, but I got no answer, I wanted to thank you with getting my career where it needed to be."

"Your welcome," I managed to choke out.

Her perfume tickled my nose and my nipples began to harden against my half-cut t-shirt.

She must have noticed my reaction because she quickly looked around to make sure no one was around to hear our little conversation.

"Can we talk after this photoshoot is over?" Lindsey asked me curiously.

"Yes, this is my last photo shoot before I head to New York tomorrow night so I will be free."

I watched as Lindsey strutted in front of the camera and waited until the makeup artist and the hair stylist gave me the okay that they were done with the touch-ups. An hour later, I began to wrap things up and hurried to put my equipment up.

No one was trying to stick around. People were tired as fuck and were ready to get the fuck out of there. I grabbed my keys to my car and was just about to head out the door when Lindsey caught up to me.

"Which hotel are you staying at?" She asked me.

"I'm staying at the Shangri- La Hotel. You can ride with me," I told her.

After Lindsey had slid into my car, I cruised through the heavy traffic towards my hotel. Twenty minutes later we had made it to the Shangri- La and was heading up the elevator towards the third floor.

No words were spoken to one another until we had closed the door to my hotel room. Lindsey walked over to my bed, kicked her shoes off, and sat on top of the covers.

"Did Carter come along?" I asked her curiously as I poured us some vodka and juice in a cup.

"No, he's keeping Charity."

"How have things been going with you?"

"Things are fine. I still can't stop thinking about you. I find myself dreaming of you every night," Lindsey admitted.

"Do Carter know this?"

"Carter knows everything. We tried working our marriage out but failed miserably. It isn't him, it's me. I can't get over you. There was nothing that Carter could do to make me happy. Karly, I haven't been happy since you and I went our separate ways. I can't live like this any longer, I can't live without you, I thought I could do it, but I can't. I love Charity with all my heart and I love Carter as well, but I'm not in love with him and he knows this. I requested a photo shoot with you because I wanted to see you again, to beg for your forgiveness for walking away from what we could have had. I came here to give you this…"

I watched as Lindsey dug inside her Louis Vuitton bag. She pulled out some papers and handed them to me. I stared at her and she ushered for me to read them.

I read the first paragraph and stared at her in astonishment. We filed for a divorce and it has just been finalized. We have joint custody of Charity. I get her every weekend and still pick her up from school every single day like it used to be. I got my own apartment and Charity spends the nights with me whenever she chooses.

I stood there with my mouth hung wide open.

Lindsey walked over to me, grabbed my drink out my hand, and sat it down on the counter.

"I love you, Karly, I'm ready to take this shit to the next level."

For six whole months, I had barely been able to function because not only did I lose the one woman I wanted to be with, but I lost my friend as well. As I stared down at Lindsey, I saw nothing but love and devotion in her eyes.

"I just want us to pick up where we left off. Can you do that for me?" Lindsey asked me.

"We can do so much better than that," I whispered into her ear.

The End

CONNECT WITH ME ON SOCIAL MEDIA

Subscribe to my mailing list by visiting my website:

https://www.shaniceb.com/

- **Like my Facebook author page:**

https://www.facebook.com/ShaniceBTheAuthor/?ref=aymt_homepag

e_panel

- **Join my reader's group on Facebook. I post short stories and sneak peeks of my upcoming novels that I'm working on**

https://www.facebook.com/groups/1551748061561216/

- **Send me a friend request on Facebook:**

https://www.facebook.com/profile.php?Id=100011411930304&_nodl

- **Follow me on Instagram:**

https://www.instagram.com/shaniceb24/?hl=en

About The Author

Shanice B was born and raised in Georgia. At the age of nine years old, she discovered her love for reading and writing. At the age of ten, she wrote her first short story and read it in front of her classmates, who fell in love with her wild imagination. After graduating high school, Shanice decided to pursue her career in Early Childhood Education. After giving birth to her son, Shanice decided it was time to pick up her pen and get back to what she loved the most.

She is the author of over twenty books and is widely known for her bestselling four-part series titled Who's Between the Sheets: Married to A Cheater. Shanice is also the author of the three-part series, Love Me If You Can, and three standalone novels titled Stacking It Deep: Married to My Paper, A Love So Deep: Nobody Else Above you, and Love, I Thought You Had My Back. In November of 2016, Shanice decided to try her hand at writing a two-part street lit series titled Loving My Mr. Wrong: A Street Love Affair. Shanice resides in Georgia with her family and her six-year-old son.

NOW AVAILABLE ON AMAZON!!!!

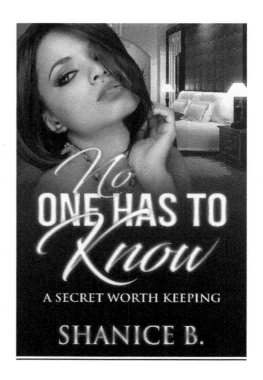

"Sometimes when you think you know a person, that's when you learn that you never knew them at all."

Layla and her brother Lamar have always been close, but their relationship soon starts to become rocky when Layla leaves her abusive boyfriend and moves in with Lamar and his girlfriend, Promise. Lamar believes he's doing the right thing by stepping in and helping his baby sister, but he soon will see that he has made a fatal mistake.

When Promise learns that her boyfriend Lamar has cheated on her, Promise feels as if her perfect world has been shattered right before her eyes. As she tries to mend her broken heart, she soon realizes that this will not be an easy task because she can't let go of the pain of her man hurting her.

Promise and Layla are both having a hard time coping with their love lives. They both feel as if they don't have anyone in their corner to help them get through their difficult time. When they realize that they're all each other have, an unlikely friendship begins to bloom that is unbreakable.

After a sultry night involving too many drinks, their close friendship turns into a hot steamy love affair.

They both know if Lamar ever finds out about their secret, all hell will break loose, but they will soon conclude that what Lamar don't know can't hurt him. Will Promise and Layla be able to keep their love a secret or will Lamar recognize the red flags that symbolize something just isn't

right?

<u>NOW AVAILABLE ON AMAZON!!!!</u>

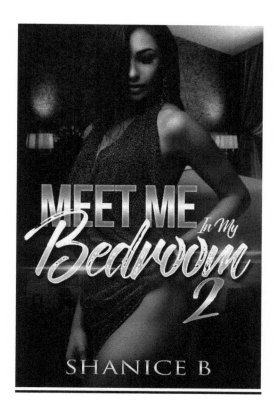

Meet Me In My Bedroom Volume 2 is a collection of erotic love stories that will pull you in from the very first page. These erotic stories are all hot steamy reads that are centered around romantic relationships. Volume

2 will make your panties wet and have you begging for more. Read at your own risk. Enjoy!!!

NOW AVAILABLE ON AMAZON!!!

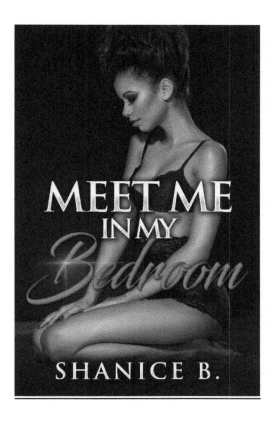

Meet Me In My Bedroom will have you glued to your Kindle from the very first page.

These erotic love stories are steamy hot reads that are centered around romantic relationships.

Each love story is jaw dropping and will have you begging for more.

SHANICE B.

Read at your own risk. Enjoy

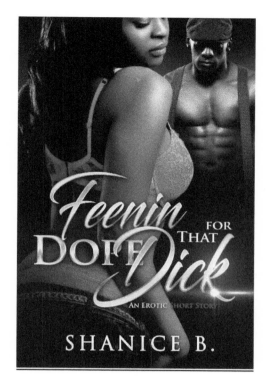

QUICK NOTE: This is a twelve-thousand-word erotic short story. If you are looking for something sexy and quick to read, then this will be the perfect read for you.

Heartbroken over her ex leaving her for another woman, Kira seems to not be able to shake her bruised ego. When Kira's best friend Shonda persuades her to have a girl's night out to take her mind off her heartbreak, Kira's life will forever be changed.

walks Jacolby...

When Kira and Jacolby lock eyes on each other their burning desire and lust for one another is what they feel. Kira is FEENIN' for some dope dick and Jacolby just happens to be the man who is eager to please her inside and outside of the bedroom.

Once Jacolby dicks her down, Kira finds herself falling for him hard and fast and there is nothing she can do about it but let it happen.

When Kira's ex magically reappears, she must make a decision. Will she go back to the man that has broken her heart or will she remain with the one man who has swept her off her feet and made her feel things she has never felt before?

CPSIA information can be obtained
at www.ICGtesting.com
Printed in the USA
LVHW091620220219
608477LV00002B/160/P